BLACK LIBRARY CELEBRATION 2023

After you enjoy the stories in this anthology, we recommend the following titles:

CADIAN HONOUR
Justin D Hill

TRAITOR ROCK
Justin D Hill

DOMINION
Darius Hinks

GODEATER'S SON
Noah Van Nguyen

HORUS RISING
Dan Abnett

WARHAMMER™
HORROR

GOTHGHUL HOLLOW
Anna Stephens

WARHAMMER™
CRIME

BLOODLINES
Chris Wraight

THE VORBIS CONSPIRACY
Various authors

BLACK LIBRARY CELEBRATION 2023

Justin D Hill, Noah Van Nguyen,
Michael F Haspil, David Annandale
& Jude Reid

A BLACK LIBRARY PUBLICATION

'The Place of Pain and Healing', 'Monsters',
'Amor Fati' and 'The Vintage' first published digitally in 2021.
'Unnatural Causes' first published in *Sanction & Sin* in 2021.
This edition published in Great Britain in 2022 by
Black Library, Games Workshop Ltd., Willow Road,
Nottingham, NG7 2WS, UK.

Represented by: Games Workshop Limited – Irish branch,
Unit 3, Lower Liffey Street, Dublin 1,
D01 K199, Ireland.

10 9 8 7 6 5 4 3 2 1

Produced by Games Workshop in Nottingham.
Cover illustration by Darren Tan.

A CIP record for this book is available from the British Library.

ISBN 13: 978-1-80026-273-7

Printed and bound by CPI Group (UK) Ltd, Croydon, CR0 4YY

CONTENTS

The Place of Pain and Healing

Justin D Hill

I

A century before, these rough wool fibres had been shorn from giant yaks on the planet of Fenris. They had been rubbed, steam-pressed and boiled in successive rounds of rigorous processing till the individual fibres had matted into one impenetrable military-grade felt. The sections of felt served a small but vital role, as dampers in the magazines of the Space Wolves Chapter's void fleet. But now the strike cruiser's magazines in which they reside are empty. The pallets of fyceline propellant are bare, the cartridges spent in massive broadsides, and the piles of disused felt are stacked in the corner of one magazine aboard Alpha IX, *Fang of Fenris,* where they act as crude bedding for the dirt-smeared form of Whiteshield Minka Lesk.

Minka lies pale and still and dirt-smeared. She might be a corpse, but for the occasional sign of life. A twitch, a flicker of eyelids, a half-formed word that could be alarm, or anger, or fear.

Or all of those together, for during the battle there was no time to make sense of what she was going through. The Battle of Cadia is a tangle of nightmare moments, twisted and bound and tightened into an ugly, cancerous lump. But now her brain starts to tug at the loose ends, trying to unravel it, trying to process it all.

To sanitise the insane.

In one dream she is squatting in the sally port of the eastern gates of Kasr Myrak, hundreds of other Whiteshields around her – packed like sheep, clutching their lasrifles in trembling fingers. The skies of Cadia have always been a nightmare bruise of swirling purple – as the Eye of Terror stared down at them – and they have grown up thinking that there could be no worse a sight. But now they know that they were wrong.

Hell has vomited a host of spiked and barnacled and rusted hulks into orbit above them. The skies are thick with enmity, and searchlights illuminate faces, tentacles and screaming maws of fanged teeth howling despair down onto the planet.

This is something they will tell their grandchildren of, if they live... which looks doubtful at this particular moment, because the Black Fleet smothers Cadia like a swarm of cockroaches, blotting out light and hope and any chance of reinforcement. The dark sky strobes with fire and lance-strikes as it hails its fury down at the planet.

Minka and the other Whiteshields have never experienced anything like this. The void shield bubble crackles and fizzes as energy trails ground themselves. But they know enough to know that this is just a prelude, a prologue, a preliminary, a preparation.

The enemy's gunners are seeking a weak point, and the tension builds as the void generators whine with effort. Above the Western Bastion, the blue bubble fails with a *pop* of pressure. Klaxons wail. Flames leap up, and a sudden lightning storm hammers down. Eruptions rip through the whole massive edifice, and then the thin blue shell of the void shield returns. But even the commanders are rattled. Their vox-enhanced voices carry over the huddled heads of the Whiteshields. Medicae teams run past them, shouting instructions to one another.

The casualties are clearly severe. Units are already being redeployed. The shock trooper platoons next to them move off along the barricades.

'Fill the gap!' The order goes out and the Whiteshields shuffle sideways. Their lines stretch thinner. They're on their own now.

The onslaught drags on. The stress becomes too much for some. They cry out in terror, weep silently or fire wild shots into the night sky.

'Hold fire!' Another order goes out, and grim discipline returns. But each time the void shields crackle, Minka is sure they will fail. She is beyond terrified. She presses her eyes closed, tries to recite her catechism, to recall things her mother told her, to run through the many codes of her Whiteshield training. But she is shaking so much her teeth rattle within her skull and she cannot get the words out. It is all she can do to hold on to her lasrifle.

In desperation she reaches inside her flak armour. Her fingers close over the items within, and she presses them into her palm. The hard metal shapes are deeply familiar. One is an autorifle hard round; the other is a cheap press-metal image of Saint Katherine picked up on a scholam field trip to the Adepta Sororitas abbey, perching on the crags above Kasr Batrok.

She prays to Saint Katherine of the Order of Our Martyred Lady and feels a moment's calm spread through her body. She focuses on this moment of calm, and at last her teeth come to rest, and the words start to tumble out.

She prays with a fervency she has never known before. She doesn't ask for much.

'Just let it begin,' she begs, and petitions for courage and strength and a clean end, when it should come. 'And let me take a heretic with me,' she asks. It is a little thing to trouble a saint with. It is all she dares to hope for. 'Saint Katherine, please do not let me die a Whiteshield.'

There is another devastating lance-strike hitting the outer defences, and suddenly a whole section of wall lifts up into the air as tunnel mines erupt along its length. The blast throws her down onto her face. They're all struggling to get up as a whistle blows and the call goes out: 'Breach! Breach!'

And then that dream ends as suddenly as a human life. And another begins.

Minka is weeks into the battle. She is lying on a pile of rubble with the crumbled edifices of habs rising up on either side. She is in the ruins of her city, Kasr Myrak.

'Shock troops', they are called, but it seems that all they are doing is falling back from one brief defensive point to another.

Las-bolts stitch the air above her head. She hunkers face down in the rubble. They have dubbed the army of heretics and penal convicts 'the Unnamed'. It's better to put a moniker to them. To separate yourself from them. To draw clear lines of distinction. But there are hundreds of thousands of them, and a few hundred are clambering over the barricade Minka abandoned twenty seconds ago, just fifty yards up the remains of Brewhouse Straat.

And she has to kill as many of them as she can, before they kill her.

Above her, to the left, comes the resonant *thud-thud* of a heavy bolter team, firing through the remains of the eponymous brewhouse. The bass-note rattle dislodges a stream of dust from the loose debris. Brass shells clatter down through the ruins. The stink of alcohol mixes with fyceline and ozone. The rockcrete dust catches in her throat.

Through the smoke and flames, she searches for a target.

She picks a man crossing the intersection. His head is hunched as if he's running into a storm. So much about him is familiar – scuffed and torn fabric boots, scavenged flak armour, Munitorum-issue overalls. He looks like he spent a past life as factorum labourer. She lines him up in her scope, and he looks up, as if he senses her staring at him. For a moment she looks him in the face and recoils. His face is a mask of horror. She takes it all in – the tattoos, the piercings, his lipless mouth, the scream of hatred.

The salvo strikes true, but the cultist does not falter. He leaps over dead and burning bodies, a bloodstained knife in his fist, powering towards her, spittle flying from the corners of his mouth.

Minka keeps her finger on the trigger till the stream of las-bolts blinds her.

Ten feet from her, he falls. She can hear him cursing and snarling. She wants to finish him off, but there's no time because another face leers up where he has been. This time the face is of a girl her own age, her scalp crudely shaved, her humanity defaced with heretical symbols carved into her bleeding cheeks.

Wake!

A boot roughly nudges Minka. The voice is muffled and distant, the accent almost unintelligible. *Girl, wake! Wake!*

The voice is insistent. But it comes to her as if through a layer of ice.

Minka cannot respond. She knows her duty, even in her dreams. In her mind there is a battle to fight. A planet to save. A verdict to overturn. And in her dreams heretic after heretic assails her. Men. Women. Minors.

The fighting becomes so desperate that the battle is reduced to bayonet work – the most terrible form of battle. The fight is all instinct, terror-lent strength, training. Her enemy are mad with battle-stimms. Their dying fingers loosen their grip from about her throat as she drives the blade in. But she is Cadian and drilled, and she fights harder and with discipline. The terror grips just as close, even in a dream, and she twitches and moans under the heavy felt sheets. And then it is all too much, even for her sleeping mind, and for solace it reaches back to before the Black Crusade.

II

Minka is sitting on a hillside, propped up against her backpack. The Black Crusade will not happen for three or more years and this moment is like a soothing balm, a drawn breath, a blessing. But it is more than that: this is a moment of hope and possibility because her team have reached the final and Minka hangs on the instructor's every word.

His name is Burgozi. War has chewed him up and spat him out again. He's missing an eye and part of his nose, one hand and two fingers off the other, and his torso is criss-crossed with scars. It looks as though parts of his body have been zipped back together. But he stands before them, hands on hips.

'This is your first live-round training,' he calls out through scarred lips. He lifts an autorifle in his hand and disengages the magazine, flicks a hard round out with the stump of his middle finger, and holds it up between thumb and stump. 'Hard round, ferro-polymer. Twenty-two calibre. If it hits you in the wrong place, this can kill.'

He lets those words sink in. Minka nods. So do the rest of her team as he explains the rules. This is Cadia, everything is serious. But even as she listens and nods, Minka's young mind wanders. Under her palm she feels the wiry hill grass.

And then the talk is over. Burgozi slips the round back into the magazine, and slams the magazine back into the rifle.

'Right. Prize goes to the team that get first blood.'

The rival team are from Kasr Batrok. They are confident, assured, patient as they file off down the hill. They have a couple of sniper-trained members, still wearing their camouflage suits of grass and lichen.

'Think they're trying to trick us?' Darage, the lad next to her, says. He's young, like her, with dark hair. They've been on camp for two weeks now, and he has not shaved, and a few strands of fluff jut out from his chin and upper lip.

Minka watches the other team and shakes her head. She doesn't know if they're trying to spook them, but she knows that Kasr Batrok is richer, bigger and better-defended than Kasr Myrak – and she feels both the pressure and the sense that they are the underdogs.

'We'll show them,' she tells Darage.

They have till nightfall to play this out. The tension builds as the day wears on. Minka's leading the flanking team. She's lying on her front at the base of a tree when she sees something in the mist ahead. She waits, then aims and fires. She doesn't even consider that she might be about to wound another Cadian. This has been her life, and this is just another form of training.

As soon as her salvo ends, she shifts position.

Just in time. One of the other band returns fire. Minka presses herself down as tracers hiss overhead. Her magazine is still hot from the recent firing. And then there is silence.

Minutes tick by. Minka's palms are wet. Her body aches. She crawls forward, desperate for a glimpse of her enemy. And then someone punches her in the left leg. It is sudden and unexpected. She spins about, thinking it is that idiot Grazon, but no one is there, and it takes a moment for the understanding to dawn.

She has been shot. *She* is the first blood.

All the realisations take a moment to process as she closes her eyes. The instructor lifts the whistle and blows a single note.

Then the shock kicks in. A medic crouches over Minka's leg, cutting away the trouser and exposing the wound. 'Tell me your name,' the medic says as she presses a needle into Minka's thigh. The woman keeps asking her questions as the suppressants take effect.

Minka is too shaken to speak. She gets a first sight of the wound and she feels sick. But nothing makes her as sick as the sight of the Kasr Batrok team standing to congratulate each other.

Minka cannot look her teammates in the eye. The medic sees the pain in her eyes. 'Next time,' she tells her.

III

Her dream tips her straight back to the moment the tunnel mines ripped through the curtain walls. 'Breach!' the shout goes as fragments of rockcrete fly up into the air. A storm of whistles blow as Minka pushes herself back up, grabs her lasrifle and slings it over her shoulder, scrambling over the rubble. The earth is breaking as the spiralling teeth of assault drills surface within the wall and assault doors slam down and heretics swarm out.

Minka grasps a length of rebar embedded in the debris and uses it to haul herself forwards. A moment later she's halfway up a treacherous tumble of rock and scree, and she must get to the top before the swarming heretics. Shrapnel rips through the smoke and dust. Las-bolts hiss through the air. Minka scrambles upwards. Her mouth is full of dust and grit.

Darage is stronger than her. He pushes forward, loses his footing, and sets off an avalanche of debris which buries him alive.

Minka is next. The way to the top lies along a slab of shattered battlements, as long and thick as a cargo-12. She steps upon the slab and it tilts. The rock is so finely balanced that it moves beneath her weight. She can hear the heretics and she is rigid with terror as the rock trembles with her.

You are a coward, she tells herself in disgust. No one is harder on herself. But fear is human, and humanity is what she fights for. And fighting is what she has been raised to do.

A mortar shell lands behind her. There are shouts of impatience and pain and terror. Minka can hear the ragged cries of the Unnamed on the other side of the ruins. She cannot wait. This is a deadly race to reach the ridgeline. She clambers higher as a face looms up from the other side.

She has made it just in time.

Minka fires, point-blank, and sees close up what a las-bolt does to a human face.

IV

Girl, wake! the voice comes again, but Minka cannot leave as her memories funnel her towards Cadia's final moments. She stands alone, holding up the broken form of Captain Rath Sturm as the world starts to crack, and warp spawn pour through the rents in reality.

The clouds swirl over her head and in the air above, something dreadful is materialising. It is a malevolent form, an apparition of hell, and Minka knows that there is no way she can fight it. Dread flows off it like smoke. Daemonfire flickers up its naked torso.

She reaches for the image of Saint Katherine hanging about her neck as its clawed hands reach out. In the palms are the faces of men and women and children that Minka knows. They are her neighbours, friends, family, and their screaming mouths are filled with flaming maggots that overflow and drip towards her.

The claws are brass brigandine. The scales rattle with the sound of chattering teeth. Of a tossed skull sliding down a bloody heap.

She holds the press-metal image, and shouts back in defiance.

V

A death rattle sounds through the *Fang of Fenris*, outnumbered as plasma generators strain to keep life-support systems running.

In the debris field of St Josmane's Hope, a motley picket of armoured frigates and merchantmen lie in ambush. They are deformed by allegiance to the Ruinous Powers, a midnight host of gnarled and pitted battle cruisers, daemonic battle monitors trailing scraps of broken chains and void-embalmed cadavers impaled upon their blighted superstructures.

Each time the Space Wolves cruiser's lance batteries fire, the corridors and hangars are thrown into darkness. Superheated oxygen burns like promethium, filling corridors with death. Fist-sized globules of molten steel cut through bulkhead and flesh, while the vacuum of space turns those exposed to it, within seconds, into ghastly husks of frozen and dehydrated flesh. Systems fail in sparks and flames, and the heretic fleet surges forward, sensing an easy kill.

It is an unfair match.

The Astartes cruiser is wounded, surrounded and outnumbered, but it smashes through the bleeding wreckage of heretic jackals. It flees for the Mandeville point, plumes of atmosphere and smoke swirling in its wake as survivors are dragged down to the medicae hall.

It is a gloomy space set deep in the heart of the strike cruiser: the lumens light a scene of misery and pain, the stillness broken by the hiss of blood pumps, amputation saws, the crackle of cauterising irons, the moans of the wounded trapped in amniotic dreams. Casualties have long since overflowed the main chamber and the corridors surrounding it, and Medicae Birgir picks his way through them. Their pale faces stare up at him as breath steams from his grille-vents. Here and there he pauses, his augmetics plugging into the data-sockets and case histories scrolling in his ocular feed.

'Lord medicae!' a voice calls.

Birgir turns as Chapter-thrall Hallr limps towards him. The failed Space Wolves aspirant is a misshapen lump, his body hunched and muscle-bound, his jutting face malformed with the failed gene-splicing. But there is a keen, angry light in his blue eyes.

'There is a problem!' he hisses through fanged teeth.

Birgir has been running on stimms for months. It takes a moment for him to recall the details. Hallr is in charge of the two stowaways. The two Cadians. Brought from the planet by Brother Skarp-Hedin.

Birgir pauses. He is weary beyond belief, but this is how he fights for the Imperium, keeping warriors alive for the next battle.

He nods, and speaks in a voice faint with exhaustion. 'I will come and see.'

The superstructure groans and buckles as Birgir follows Hallr through the corridors to the magazine. Power has been diverted from the habitable levels to keep the strike cruiser's shields alive.

Only critical life-support systems are still running. The air is thin, their breaths steam in the darkness. The walls gleam with a film of frost, icicles stabbing down from the low metal ceilings, glittering in the darkness of the shell-chamber's vaulting.

Birgir had never seen the magazine empty before. He stands in wonder, looking about him. The stink of fyceline hangs in the chamber, but there is not a single charge left.

'This way,' the Chapter-thrall says and points towards a distant point of light where the two humans from Cadia are lying on a bed of felt mats. They make their way towards them.

Medicae Birgir bends over the first. It is a male. His mechadendrite feels its way across the skull-plate. It finds the data-socket. A spool of medical information floods into Birgir's data-banks.

Captain Rath Sturm. Formerly 101st Airborne, promoted to 94th Kasrkin.

The medical notes stored within the skull-mounted data-spool are typical for a veteran warrior. There's all manner of documentary evidence. Sex, name, number, rank, unit, survival assessment rates, and a spool of addenda that have been added by medicaes over the years: minor injuries, organ trouble, a series of precancerous rad-boils that had been removed, biopsied and cauterised.

As Medicae Birgir runs through the information, his shoulder-mounted mechadendrites pull the felt bedding aside and he assesses the captain's current health. There are numerous cuts, severe bruises and abrasions, laser burns, field-treated impact wounds and three oblique anterior fractures in the lower three sternovertebral ribs.

Nothing life-threatening.

A severe shot of stimms brings the captain suddenly awake. He groans with pain as he takes a breath. He sounds like a drowning man reaching air, gulping in panic.

'What is your name?' Birgir asks.

Sturm moans. Birgir repeats his question, but the man clutches Birgir's arms and sucks in shallow breaths.

'What is your name, trooper?' he asks.

There is a long pause before at last the answer comes to the man. 'It is Rath. Rath Sturm. Captain Rath Sturm.'

'Can you move your arms?' The medicae's voice is flat. 'I need you to answer me. Are you hurt? Is this your blood?'

'Some of it. That hurts,' Sturm says with a hiss as Birgir finishes his checks.

'Understood,' the medicae replies. 'This will take your pain.' A needle slides into Sturm's arm and administers a direct dose of suppressants, vitamins and nutrients. 'Well done, captain,' he says as he moves on to the next bed.

The female is not much more than a girl. She is stiff beneath the sheets. His mechadendrites assess her vital statistics. There is a burn down the middle of her palm, and numerous other cuts, burns, abrasions – but there are no life-threatening injuries. All are healing as expected, except for the fact that her heart is running at a hundred and thirty beats per minute and her blood pressure is dangerously high.

A mechadendrite lifts her eyelid while another shines a light into her eye. No pupillary dilation in either eye. He runs through a series of tests, but there is no response. She twitches and moans.

Chapter-thrall Hallr has spent hours watching her and there is fear in his eyes. 'Is she possessed?' he whispers.

The medicae shakes his head. He has seen many things since he left the icy plains of Fenris, but this girl is something of a mystery.

'Can you wake her?' Hallr demands.

Birgir is wary of giving her too much, but nothing else works. At last he says, 'I will give her a short measure.'

The stimms do not take long to kick in. Minka sits bolt upright. Her eyes blink suddenly open, and she sucks in a deep breath, like one surfacing at last from deep, deep water.

'Girl. What is your name?'

She cannot get enough oxygen into her lungs. The medicae puts a hand to her shoulder and she flinches.

'I am Medicae Birgir. You are safe. Can you tell me your name?'

Minka's muscles are tense. She is hyperventilating, her hands flailing.

'Calm,' he tells her. 'You are safe. Tell me your name and rank. Tell me where you fought. Is this your blood?'

She pushes him away.

'You are aboard the *Fang of Fenris*,' he tells her. 'You are safe. You need to eat and drink. I am Medicae Birgir. You are safe. Can you tell me your name? Calm,' he repeats. 'Speak. Tell me your name and rank. Tell me where you fought. Are you bleeding?'

She cannot answer, and Birgir cannot stay.

Time passes. She cannot get enough oxygen into her lungs. Panic rises within her and she starts to moan in shock. There are no words to express what she feels. She remembers and her agony is a dreadful raw, animal sound.

Rath knows exactly how she feels. He drags himself from under the felt matting, and pulls himself across the frozen decking. Her body is stiff and unyielding. He holds her as the waves of shock and grief run through her. He ignores the pain in his ribs as she struggles against him.

'Breathe slowly,' he tells her as she starts to retch as the tremors eventually slow. 'They're just dreams.' He holds her close. 'Hush,' he says. 'It's over.'

'What's wrong with me?' she rasps.

'It's the stimms,' Rath tells her.

'I feel awful,' she says. Her teeth rattle as she shivers convulsively. 'Was he trying to poison me?'

Rath laughs and it makes him wince. 'He had to bring you back.'

'Throne!' she says, and starts to retch again. All that comes out is a thin black bile. She wipes the strands away and spits the taste out. 'I dare not lie down.'

'You should.'

She is pale and sweating. 'I had terrible dreams.'

'They're just dreams,' Rath says again. He does not sound like he believes himself. She looks away, and her eyes fall on the misshapen form of Hallr. She looks away again and thinks, *Look what the Imperium has done to us all.*

She remembers Instructor Burgozi from her Whiteshield days, and what his service had done to him. The missing fingers, the scars, the sense of having failed. She feels tears start to well up. Her throat tightens, her lips press together, and she bites her tongue as she tries to hold them back. She tastes blood but she does not allow those tears to fall. She takes a deep breath and stands up. The truth is she dare not close her eyes because she knows what terrors lie there.

She whispers, 'We lost, didn't we?'

His throat is too tight to speak. All he can do is nod. Now, as far as either of them know, they are the only two Cadians left alive, and they have failed their millennia-long trust.

This pain they share is worse than living.

It is a long time before Minka can speak. 'We should have died.'

He nods slowly.

* * *

VI

Minka has been walking for hours. She is in the seventh emptied shell-chamber when the voice speaks to her. It is deep and sonorous, and it reverberates through the dark chamber.

She freezes.

She had thought she was alone, but as she turns, she sees a giant is standing only a few yards from her. He is so large and square that it feels as though a wall has just spoken to her. It seems impossible that someone of such size would move so silently. But he is there.

A Space Marine, not dressed in battleplate, but in a black fabric, studded with metal plugs about his chest and arms and legs. Her eyes pick details out from the darkness. Tall, rangy despite a hyper-developed musculature, an over-large face, beard plaited and twined with beads and bones.

He speaks again. 'You are recovered.'

She has to shake herself before she can speak. 'Yes,' she stutters.

He crouches down. Even so, his face is higher than hers. He has the same monobrow that Hallr has. It gives his deep-set eyes a bestial and serious look. His face is so large, she thinks, it's like looking at an ogryn.

'It is I, Skarp-Hedin. You walked straight past me.'

She pauses to consider. So much has happened but the name is familiar, and then she remembers. It is the Space Wolf who brought her and Rath up from the planet.

'You look well,' he says.

'I am.'

He nods slowly. 'You are Cadian?'

She has always said this with pride, but now she hesitates before answering. 'Yes. I am. Well, I was.'

'Was?'

She nods.

'Either you are Cadian, or you are not.'

She hesitates. 'But we failed.'

His mouth is closed, but the tips of fangs protrude from under his closed lips. He nods thoughtfully, as if savouring her words. His presence is so awesome she feels compelled to speak just to fill the silence.

'I find myself doubting everything that I have been told.'

'And what were you told?'

'We were the gatekeepers. We held the madness at bay. It was a heavy task, but my forefathers never failed. But now. Cadia. It's gone.' She looks at him, doubting her own sanity. 'It has gone, hasn't it?'

It is hard to judge how old the Astartes are, but Skarp-Hedin's ice-blue eyes are old and wise, and there is sadness buried within them. But he does not answer.

'Cadia – it broke. Yes?'

'Yes.'

'So we lost.'

'Lost?'

'Yes. The Cadian Gate. All of it,' she says, as if this were obvious, but then words fail her.

'"Lost". I do not know this word.' He smiles and she realises he is joking, but his smile is a terrifying sight: his oversized mouth opens to a maw of fangs. 'You have a short life, Cadian. Mine is likely to be a little longer. At night on my world, when I was a boy, I would sit and look up at the night sky, and occasionally there were streaks of light. Stars, falling from the void. The best we can hope for is a short flash of brilliance. Some of us burn a little longer, and brighter, than others. If you think that you have lost, then it will be so. But you are here talking to me! And you are alive, and as long as you can fight, the battle is not over.'

She pauses. At last she says, 'So… we keep fighting?'

'Why would you stop?' he says.

She thinks on this and remembers that day when she was shot in the leg. She remembers the arrogance of the Kasr Batrok Whiteshields. And she remembers the look on the medic's face as she bandaged her leg. 'Next time,' she'd said to her. And she was right. A year later the two teams met again in the final, and this time it was the Kasr Myrak team who won the bout.

Being Cadian, she thinks, is about more than a bloodline or a planet. It is a mindset and a method: to fight and to advance, whatever the odds.

She starts to speak, but he puts up his hand, and sniffs the air. She strains the darkness to try and gauge what he has sensed; feels nothing for a long time, but he is clearly listening to something beyond her.

'We have reached the Mandeville point, Upsilon Nine,' he says.

'And what is that?'

'It is the point where we transition into the warp.'

'What is the warp?'

He pauses. 'It is a way of moving through space. To fold distance.'

She nods as she adds this to her learning. Then she feels the transition in the pit of her stomach and it makes her feel sick.

There is a long pause. Skarp-Hedin closes his eyes. 'It is done,' he says at last. 'They are out there, searching for our souls. Can you feel them?'

She shakes her head.

He looks about. 'No matter. They are there. They will *always* be there. As long as there is someone to fight, then there is yet hope for humanity. That grit that allowed your people to defend your home world for ten thousand years. *That* is your inheritance. You must pass it on.' He pauses, listening – but not to her – and then stands suddenly. 'I am needed.'

He turns abruptly and starts to stride away. His footsteps are silent. With each stride he fades into the darkness, and leaves her standing alone.

Minka calls out after him. 'Space Wolf. Where are we going?'

He does not turn, but his voice comes back to her. 'I cannot tell you.'

Minka pauses and takes in a deep breath. The stimms are starting to wear off, at last. 'I suppose there will be another battle to fight.'

His distant voice is a rumble. 'While you are alive, there is always another battle.'

A flash of understanding runs through her. She is not just the end of a great fighting legacy; she will also be its beginning.

VII

Minka retraces her steps through the cavernous magazines of the strike cruiser. She has been walking for hours. She is deathly tired when she sees the pile of felt mats in the dim light.

Hallr has gone and Rath is alone. He is asleep. She lies down and uses both hands to pull one of the heavy mats on top of her. It is ingrained with grease and the stains of spilt unguents. It's a distinctively military scent as its weight presses down upon her. It is the odour of quartermasters' offices and Militarum storage facilities from Fenris to Armageddon, Cadia to the Eastern Fringe. It is a smell that reminds her of Cadia, and her father.

As soon as she closes her eyes, the stink of the mats colours her unconscious. In her dreams she is knee-high in her childhood hab. Her mother cleans each part of her lasrifle and lays them all out on the table. She's threading the barrel back onto the stock when her father comes home. He is dead tired. His face is pale, his hands and jacket ingrained with military unguents. But he will not rest.

'Come,' he tells Minka, and puts out a hand and takes hers in his.

It is a sacred night on Cadia, when the unnamed dead are remembered, where those without graves are honoured. Incinerator bins are burning around the perimeter of the kasr walls, the silhouettes of Cadians standing around them, dark against the flames. Her father leads her to the broad rockcrete stairs, worn into trenches by generations of Cadians before her.

Each bowed step is an effort for one so small, but at last they reach the top and he leads her up onto the broad firing platform. She turns and the pillbox habs have all fallen away behind them and she feels the wind against her cheeks.

'Come here,' he says, and lifts her up in both hands. She looks up but she does not see falling stars, only the Eye of Terror, a baleful bruise in the night sky, glaring down at her.

'Tell them!' her father hisses, and she knows what she has to say. It is the word she learnt from her parents, and they from theirs before, all the way back to the first settlement of the planet.

'Never!' her memory-self shouts at the Eye of Terror.

A decade later Cadia will fall, but not Minka. She has bled, but she still stands, and she waits.

For next time.

YOUR NEXT READ

CADIAN HONOUR
by Justin D Hill

Sent to the capital world of Potence, Sergeant Minka Lesk and the Cadian 101st discover that though Cadia may have fallen, their duty continues.

Monsters

Noah Van Nguyen

Yndrasta was coming in too fast.

Through gusts of wind and gouts of rain, the Shyishan hill swelled beneath her. She could make out a tor of dusk-grey stone, a baleful realmgate perched atop it. A midnight-black battle line of Stormcast Eternals held back the horrors pouring from the portal's dismal spell-light. Watching them was like watching a dark fist grip wine from a spilt cask. The gibbering tide leaked through the battle line's fingers, running over its hands.

Yndrasta grimaced. The Anvils of the Heldenhammer needed her. They needed her now.

She tucked her wings, tightened her approach, ignoring her speed. Wind buffeted her. Rain pelted her sigmarite warplate like barbarian arrows. Off her flank, the Knight-Venator and his flight of Prosecutors chased to keep up. They were Anvils of the Heldenhammer, too, dark-hearted and sombre. Stormcast like Yndrasta but only half-willing allies, pulled into her hunt by the force of her will, by the terrible gravity of her legend. They did not fear Yndrasta. For Stormcasts never feared.

But they were wary.

Before the realmgate, through slashes of rain, a Lord of Change leered. The capricious greater daemon had never been christened in mortal syllables. The shamans called it only the Anomia, the nameless one. Even the Anvils had been reluctant to face the soul-eater's tricks.

To Yndrasta, it was only prey. She was the slayer.

She dived. Her allies soared behind her and their fusillade picked up. Thrice-blessed arrows and stormcall javelins cracked like lightning into the crag-crowded hilltop, hammering back the daemonic tide. Gabbling Pink Horrors split asunder. Each ruined half morphed into a more diminutive blue daemon, weeping and morose. Then those were obliterated, and then again the things which their deaths spawned.

Ungiving, the Anvils held the hill's brow. They chanted Yndrasta's name, awaiting her arrival. She wondered if they relished the kill as she did. She wondered if it made their hearts pulse and their blood race.

Shyish bulged closer. Behind the Anomia, the baleful realmgate's components floated in eerie patterns. Soon it would activate. Unless Yndrasta killed the Anomia first, the creature would escape.

A bolt of sorcerous flame streamed just past her shoulder, scorching her pinions. An ice-white flash and the crack of thunder told her one of the Prosecutors had not made it. Yndrasta hardly noticed. The kill. There was only the kill.

The Anomia screeched. Its clawed arms began unfolding in concentric shapes. Its vulture features hardened into scabrous corners, then swirled into a storm of kaleidoscopic light. Rain-soaked plumage and mottled flesh inflated into recursive bubbles. What emerged from the mutative storm was sickening and imponderable. Wings, upon wings. Eyes, upon eyes. Discs of bronze and purposeless flame. The sight was ineffable, profound…

And pathetic. The Anomia was afraid. To protect itself, the daemon had abandoned its physical form. Now it was harmless and invulnerable.

But invulnerability wouldn't stop Yndrasta. She clenched her jaw, sheered left, barely controlling her descent. This gale reeked of malign magic, a cheap and clever defence. She wouldn't get another pass. She wouldn't make it–

She landed, hard. The maddening visage of the Anomia glared down at her from its place on the tor. Yndrasta didn't stop to admire the abomination. Elegant, efficient, she hefted her holy spear, Thengavar, to her shoulder. She transferred the momentum from her reckless landing into a run up, recruiting every muscle in her body into the coming throw. Force passed up the axis of her, from her toes through her spine to the tips of her fingers. Yndrasta heard the sound of her breath, felt the wind whip it from her lungs; she smelled the Shyishan petrichor in the rain, reeking of death, and relished its taste on her lips.

From the Stormcast battle line, orders were given to withdraw. The warriors pounded back, step by step, making way, but not for the daemons. They chanted Yndrasta's many epithets, awaited her killing blow.

And Yndrasta's throw was perfect. Thengavar, sister-in-steel to the God-King's own Ghal Maraz, flew. The glistering weapon whistled through the storm, shrinking into the Anomia's swirling mass, penetrating into…

Into its very…

Her eyes hollow, her shoulders heaving, Yndrasta scanned the Anomia's spectral mass. Thengavar had disappeared. It did not return. She had… missed.

Or Thengavar had missed? The concept felt so unreal Yndrasta wasn't even sure how to express it. She drew her runeblade. There would be a time to contemplate the impossibility of what had just happened.

First, the Anomia. She was the slayer.

Yndrasta roared and charged the maddening monstrosity upon the dais. But the ground folded beneath her, and she stumbled. Her wings flapped, but it was like flying through aether. The air was gone, sucked from the hilltop as if by bellows. A spell-trap, Yndrasta realised. Another cheap sorcerer's trick. But it had its effect, and Yndrasta tumbled into the earthen maw which opened beneath her. She plummeted.

Somewhere far above her, a sick thing laughed.

When the air finally returned, it was useless. Yndrasta barely slowed her descent with a well-timed pulse of her wings. She crashed hard into a pool. Metal clanged on stone. Water doused her. She felt ill, unable to breathe, and ripped the sigmarite bevor from her warplate. She let it dangle, gasped. The air was cool, crisp. She was alive. *Alive...*

And nowhere near her quarry.

Yndrasta shouted until she went hoarse. She punched the water's surface, soaking herself again. She had been so close. Right there, on the verge!

Water dripping from her drenched features, Yndrasta huffed and quieted, finding some pale source of calmness within her. It was a wretched, futile thing. She felt humiliated. Like a hole had been bored through the core of her and she could not cover it up. She ran her mind over those sanity-curdling moments. The Anomia, that monstrosity of flame and wings and geometrically unsound shapes. The universe folding upon itself within the baleful realmgate. Thengavar disappearing, as if it had never even been thrown.

She shook her head. The recollections made her feel as if

her soul had begun to run. Now she was compromised, half warped...

That feeling would fade. So would the humiliation. But Thengavar... Yndrasta batted at the water again. The shaman court had promised Thengavar could pierce the Anomia's wards. Either they were lying or they had been fooled. The fault was not hers. Yndrasta was not perfect, not by any stretch, but she had thrown her spear true. Thengavar did not miss.

A black mirror of knee-deep water pooled around her. The mere rippled with Yndrasta's silvered reflection. She glared at the misshapen image of herself, wondering about what she saw. A long blade of silver hair, shaved temples. Her face, snow-pale, high-cheeked. A pair of ugly scars crossing one eye from brow to jawline.

She had been broken. So many times.

So what? This was far from over. Failure changed nothing. Yndrasta had come to Shyish to slay the Anomia, and she would not leave until that was done. The kill vitalised her. It was all she lived for.

Her eyes wandered. She was in some kind of miraculous grotto beneath the ground, untouched by war despite the carnage above. The clamour of the battle on the hill echoed here, far below. She must return, lest the Anvils sell their lives for nothing. The Shyishan Stormhost made for a gloomy lot, and Yndrasta wouldn't give them more reason to pine over their dark fates and Reforged souls, or to spread more rumours of her heartlessness among the Stormcast. She was cruel, yes. But not needlessly so.

Yndrasta flexed her wings, preparing to leave, but something stayed her. A feeling. She glanced around. A tree loomed over the water. An ancient willow, its fronds stroking the surface of the void-black pool. Dead light gleamed beyond its whips of foliage, illuminating strange pixies in the grotto's air.

Yndrasta wrinkled her nose. This place smelled... unusual. Of death. And life everlasting, like the sterile corridors of Sigmaron's Soul Mills. And roasted meat.

'Sigmar?' spoke a stranger, his voice gravelly from disuse.

Yndrasta turned, her armour creaking with her gentle movement. Beneath the wizened willow, a hulking man-thing hunkered over a guttering flame. He was a big boar of a mortal, like an ogor-son, all muscle and just enough fat to provide protection from a good blade. Beside him, a strutted-up pot straddled a small fire like a Khainite cauldron in miniature.

The mortal stepped from the darkness, glaring. A tuft of braided hair dangled from his pate to his chest, black as the day the realms would die. A thick moustache weighed down his mouth, each end hanging almost to his hips, like reins on a dracoth's bit. And his skin: it was hardened and black like coal, like the charred flesh of the vermin he roasted on a bent spit beside his pot. The rocky char had worn away in some places. In the palms of his hands, the folds of his joints. Those crannies shone like burnished bronze. But what held Yndrasta's attention were his eyes. Smouldering red gems, enchanted with formidable magic.

Yndrasta tensed. Something deep within her, something immutable and untouched by her Reforgings, detected a threat. This mortal was dangerous.

He leaned in. His cliff-wide brow smoothed. 'You're not Sigmar.'

'I am Yndrasta.' Her voice was husky, overused. 'I am Sigmar's huntress and slayer. Who are you?'

The mortal's ruby-eyes lifted. He glanced to the fleshy trunk of the great willow. There, propped up against the tree, a double-headed battle-axe resplendent with power. Yndrasta could feel the pulse of its war-heart beating in her breast. She could taste its marvellous heat on the air. That was a weapon of Azyr if ever she had seen one.

The mortal's eyes returned to her.

Yndrasta raised her finger. 'Don't.'

The man-thing tumbled towards the axe like an avalanche.

Yndrasta ripped her wings through the air. She lurched up, sailing through the willow fronds, and landed gracefully between the stranger and his weapon.

He staggered to a halt. Yndrasta's drawn sword prodded into his neck, just beneath those dracoth reins. The blade's tip rasped against his coal-black skin. Beside them, the battle-axe's presence felt like a great weight. Lift it, and the world might keel over on its side, and they'd both slide off to the bottom of the universe.

'Why would Sigmar come here?' Yndrasta said.

The mortal's eyes shimmered. He had a desperate look to him. His hands seemed tense, ready to shield himself, or gouge out her eyes. Whichever he felt might save his life, Yndrasta thought.

'You're a stranger,' he said, uneasy. 'You burst into my home, armed and mantled like you came to slay godbeasts. But it's only me here. And I'd say that warrants me reaching for my woodsplitter.'

Woodsplitter. The weapon radiated the heat of dead suns.

This man – and he was a man, Yndrasta could smell his humanity like a prey-thing's spoor – was old. He stood with a wizard's stoop. An antiquated rhotic trill pattered from his tongue like a drumroll, harkening to ages Yndrasta had never known. And his burnt hide. And that bronze, like an encasement beneath the coal scars. And that axe – *worldsplitter* might be the better word…

Yndrasta had spent months hunting the Anomia. She knew well the legends which surrounded it.

'You're Voyi,' she said.

The man's scoff was like a volcanic eruption. 'No. I'm tired. Go back where you came from. Leave me alone.'

Yndrasta lifted her chin. 'When Sigmar's pantheon still ruled from Highheim, the gods had champions. Mortals, who fought in their names. Sigmar chose some fated few to lead them, as he would later choose us Stormcast. They received his blessings. From Grungni the Maker, and the God-King himself. Eyes wrought from earthfire. Or enchanted flesh, to resist the Dark Powers' corroding touch.'

'I don't like this story,' the man interrupted.

Yndrasta gave a dry laugh, but her lips were flat and her eyes were stony. 'No. I shouldn't think you would, Voyi.'

The pits in his eyes flared. Then his face smoothed. He said nothing, as if silence could make the revelation go away.

Yndrasta spared an unkind smile. 'Voyi. The Unblessed, the Traitor, whom Sigmar entrusted with the defence of Sigmaron in his hour of need, and who betrayed him. You *are* Voyi. You are the Unremembered One.'

Voyi stared. 'Not as unremembered as I'd like.'

'*I* know you,' Yndrasta said. 'From the first sagas. I'm one of the few.'

Voyi froze. 'Then you're in his confidence.'

'Yes.'

His lips pursed. 'Then you know what I know.'

Yndrasta nodded. 'He is not a forgiving god. He knows spite. He knows malice.'

'And he does not forget old slights, it seems. Even after an age.' Voyi's eyes lowered to Yndrasta's sword. 'Get on with it.'

Yndrasta shook her head. 'You defeated the Anomia in the Age of Myth. Tell me how. I'll pray mercy for you, when I tell the God-King you live.'

Doubt clouded the heat in Voyi's eyes. 'The Anomia? Am I not a fair prize?'

'I hunt monsters, not traitors,' Yndrasta said. 'The Anomia is my chosen quarry. You are nothing.'

Voyi *hmphed*. 'I'd wondered what the ruckus was. You're one of those he replaced us with. Stormcast Eternals. Didn't think I'd be so fortunate as to meet one.'

Yndrasta canted her head. 'You have a bizarre view of fortune.'

'Maybe.' Voyi chuckled. 'But there is poetry to you, eh? Monsters, hunting monsters.'

Yndrasta's features went hard as ice. 'I am no monster.'

'Yes. You are. You're the monsters he replaced us with. Loyal little thunder golems, clad in metal which is named after him.' Voyi's nostrils flared. 'The Great Enemy has daemons. Now so does he. Even picks you from among the dead. Or sometimes he saves you the trouble of dying, plucks you when you're ripe as roses.' He spat. 'That's all we are to him. Raw material.'

Yndrasta's eye twitched. It was easy to imagine betraying Voyi's survival to Sigmar. She began to think she looked forward to it. Maybe she'd even be the one sent for him. And why not? He was human, yes. But he was irksome and a renegade, and even humans could be monsters.

Voyi had power in him yet. Yndrasta could sense it, a lingering soul-link between him and that axe, warm and tensed, like his mountainous hands. She imagined how a duel between them might look. Voyi's earth-shaking blows, moments behind her lightning-fast strikes. His enchanted blood spraying her armour like baptismal waters. His charred head dangling from her warplate by that barbaric braid…

And finally, Sigmar's merciless satisfaction as she laid his skull at the base of his throne.

She could do it now. She had that prerogative.

'Tell me how you defeated it and I shall be kind,' Yndrasta said. 'My spear disappeared in its aura. How did you do it? Did you use that axe?'

'No.'

Yndrasta raised a brow. 'You were unarmed?' The shaman court had mentioned such a requirement, but they had spoken in riddles she thought she hadn't fully understood.

'I mean I won't help you,' Voyi said.

Yndrasta straightened. 'Why? To protect that creature?'

Voyi nodded. 'You get what you want, you'll just go and tell Sigmar where I am. There'll be no more hiding from him. And the Anomia gave me this sanctuary, gave me its word it would protect me.'

'That turned out as well as one might have expected,' Yndrasta said.

Voyi's features hardened. 'The daemon's better to its word than Sigmar ever was.'

Yndrasta's lips curled. Those words pierced.

'Sigmar stands alone,' she said. 'So yes, his wardenship over mankind requires difficult decisions. No one expects a heathen renegade hiding in a pocket of the world to understand that. If Sigmar betrayed your trust, he must have seen you for what you were, from the very beginning. I do.'

'Don't pretend you know a thing about me,' Voyi said. 'Sigmar's a bastard and always was. I'll not help you. Not if it's the last thing I do.' He folded his arms. 'Or... don't do. You understand.'

For the span of a held breath, Yndrasta maintained her vacant expression. Then she bent with anger and roared. Her armour rattled on her shoulders. Her blade quivered at Voyi's neck. This close, on the verge, and he dared defy her?

'If you won't help,' Yndrasta snarled, refreshing her blade grip, 'maybe I'll just kill you now. I think Sigmar might like that.'

Voyi's bold mask cracked, fear flashing across his face. He stumbled, and Yndrasta's blade followed him. He stuttered in search of words.

'I'm not afraid of dying,' he managed, firmly enough that Yndrasta thought maybe he really wasn't. 'Look around you. This is the afterlife of my people. The Black Pond, under the Judgement Willow. They came here, my fathers and sons, as ghosts. I died when they died. When Sigmar let them die. And when their laughter bled from these caves and their memory went to dust in the corners, I was as gone as they were. So kill me if you want. It's what you're made for. And you can't possibly take any more from me than Sigmar did.'

Yndrasta scoffed. 'I thought you a heathen traitor. You're only a spoilt brat. Whining about your due, after everything the God-King gave you. Everything you threw in his face.'

Voyi's scowl went slack. 'Everything? You mean everything he didn't do? Or everything he kept safe and sound in Azyr, all these ages? Pretty and eternal, just like you, even as my people went extinct! He did nothing for us. Maybe you mean everything he did for that Hag Queen, Morathi, even knowing what she was. Oh, yes. I've heard the rumours of your city, Anvilgard. The gheists made from its fall told me, passing through these cave walls in flight from Nagash. Sigmar's own city, put to Khainite slaughter by Morathi's hands. And after all he did for them.

'Yet you speak of *everything*. Perhaps you mean everything in Sigmaron, that gleaming city with all those staring statues of him. Tell me – are the lightning bolts still everywhere? They are. Oh, I see it in your eyes, they are. Made from Ghurish marble and Hyshian gems and precious Aqshy metals. You thought it all came from Azyr? Did you even care to ask? I doubt it. Because you fight his wars – and don't tell me you don't, I know you do, you're a *Stormcast Eternal!* – but you never notice! You bring the wars with you, and if they aren't there when you come, they always are when you leave.

'And as those starving mortals you claim to protect finally *die* for you, Sigmar's at least good enough to take their souls! He melts them down, recasts them in the shape of himself, just like he does with their treasures! Not subtle. But he never has been! He's a god, and you're his monsters! You didn't know, because how could you? You're too busy preening your angel feathers and polishing your shining armour and prattling of glory! You're too busy barging into old men's homes and waving your sacred swords in their faces! You won't even let me eat my supper! You're so fearsome and noble I must go hungry to witness you!'

Voyi's food was burning. The pot overboiled; the flame guttered and spat.

Yndrasta cast her gaze across the cavern. She finally saw it for what it was. A cheap refuge, built with odds and ends for a broken man with nowhere to go and no one to love him. Voyi put on a bold face and clad his indignation in sophistry, but he stood with shaking legs and a crooked back. And when Yndrasta had been angry – when she had been *angry* – fear ran through him like a current of lightning. She threatened a harmless man.

Yndrasta sheathed her blade. She had fantasised about setting Voyi's head at Sigmar's feet. He dreamed of eating roasted vermin and slurping soup boiled with the water of his extinct tribe's afterlife.

'Go and eat your food,' she said.

Voyi tromped back to his campfire, grumbling, not once looking back.

Yndrasta walked a long circle around him. Even if he wasn't pathetic, she couldn't kill him. Not yet. She must learn the Anomia's weakness. But Voyi wasn't going to help, and time was running out. The distant clamour above continued – the battle had not abated – but the Anomia's baleful realmgate could activate at any moment. Then it would be too late. Yndrasta would be left with nothing to return to her trophy halls but stinging shame and the memory of Thengavar's loss. The Anvils of the Heldenhammer would spread rumour of her failure.

And Sigmar…

He had never been a forgiving god, Yndrasta thought. She had always admired him for that. And when she killed, it was for him as much as herself. But he would not forget her failure.

Yndrasta watched Voyi settle himself to eat. She could do this. She could convince him to help her. What was it but a different kind of hunt?

'My spear,' she said. 'Thengavar. It was Sigmar's gift to me. The Anomia stole it.'

Voyi looked at her askance. 'If you tried to kill it with it, that's no wonder.'

'You fought the Anomia. You know exactly what it is. A monster. The daemon feeds on mortals' souls.'

Voyi ladled a miserable portion of mushroom-studded broth into his bowl. 'What difference is there between that and what Sigmar does? Or the Great Necromancer? Or the Twins, or the bloody Hag Queen, or any of them? They all eat souls, even if some are pickier than others. And you Stormcasts didn't make it out alive, either. Sigmar ate your souls. Look at you. You even talk like him.'

Yndrasta didn't know where to begin. 'I am exactly where I want to be, Voyi. Were you so different?'

He paused. 'No. Perhaps not. But maybe that's the problem. And I didn't stay.' He pulled meat from the carcass on the spit. 'Here.'

The corners of Yndrasta's nose rose. No part of her wanted to answer that invitation, but she was a slayer, not a savage. 'I am not your guest.'

Voyi shrugged, gnawing on the stringy meat. 'You kill things, huntress. I smell death on you, and it's not this realm. If the fact some of those things you butcher are daemons is supposed to be proof you're good, that's a low mark to set.' He swallowed. 'Even if you are special. A monster slayer, you say.'

'Not a monster, if that is your meaning.'

'Take away the lightning and the bloody armour and I wouldn't even see the difference. All you do is kill. You're like the damned Bloodbound. *Slayer.* Ha! I bet you even take heads.'

Yndrasta glared. 'That is different.'

Voyi grimaced. 'Course it is. It's always different.'

She steeled her eyes. If Voyi thought the Stormcast were monsters, he hadn't seen monsters.

'Kragnos,' she whispered.

Voyi fell still. 'You utter powerful names in dark places. Say his name and he shall appear.'

'You wanted monsters,' Yndrasta said. 'I told you – I hunt monsters. The Anomia is a minor errand. My true quarry is Kragnos, the End of Empires.' Her fists closed, her gauntlets hissing against themselves. 'I will destroy Kragnos. I yearn for it, more than anything in all the realms. Is that the desire of a monster?'

Voyi darkened. 'I told you. Monsters, hunting monsters.' He sighed and continued eating. 'If you're after Kragnos, Sigmar sent you to do what he could not. And you're a fool for listening.'

'I choose my quarry,' Yndrasta said. 'I am not Sigmar's hound. I do not fetch. He does not send me.'

Voyi shook his head. 'Yes. He does. Just by letting you go, he does. You think I don't know? I remember what it was like. Without his approval, we're nothing. And it's true. Look what happened to me.'

'You did this to yourself,' Yndrasta said. 'If you ever truly knew him, then you would know his decisions are not without reason. His choices are necessary.'

'His choices are heartless.'

'Yes.' Yndrasta's jaw was iron. 'When they have to be. When needs must. Our wars are different than yours were. To save one life, sometimes a thousand must perish. Sometimes that is the best that can be done.'

Voyi tossed the remnants of his bowl into a patch of moss. He stared. After a long breath, he nodded. 'Maybe.' He rose and pushed through the fronds, towards his axe. 'But have you ever th–'

Yndrasta moved. A gust kicked up, and her sigmarite-shod boots padded to the earth.

She was between Voyi and his axe again, her blade back at his neck.

Voyi lowered his bowl to a pile of miserable effects. 'Easy. Tidying. No more.'

Yndrasta scanned him. She sheathed her blade. 'You're wrong about him. Maybe that's why you were fool enough to betray him.'

'I didn't betray him,' Voyi said. He took Yndrasta in, head to toes, contemplating her. 'I've never sensed power like yours, nor purpose. Not in all my time in the heavens. Not in all my time in the earth.'

Finally they were getting somewhere. 'Power alone will not defeat the Anomia,' Yndrasta said. 'How, Voyi? How did you bind it?'

Voyi considered. 'Not with power. I only have shreds left of what Sigmar gave me, hardly enough to use it willy-nilly. But I could beat the Anomia again. If I had to.' His forehead crinkled and crunched. 'It's a secret. But once you know, it's easy.'

'Tell me,' Yndrasta said. 'In return I can help you. I do not know what my pleas are worth to him, but I will beg his mercy.'

Voyi whiffled. 'And you said you knew him. Tell me, huntress – what mercy is a traitor due?'

Yndrasta's features grew frosty.

'I've a better idea,' Voyi said. 'Keep this place and my survival a secret, and I'll help.' He extended his hand. 'Whatever is spoken of me, I'm a man of my word. What are you?'

Yndrasta glared at his burnt fingers. What was the worth of a traitor's word? And would she be any better than him, to conceal his survival from Sigmar? Sigmar still craved vengeance against Voyi. He did not speak of him, and he had struck his name from the chronicles, but he had not forgotten.

Few knew the God-King's will as well as Yndrasta. Few knew the cruelty of it.

'I cannot lie to the God-King,' Yndrasta said. 'Not for you.'

Voyi shuddered, as if the burns on his enchanted skin were still fresh, the pain still real. He withdrew his hand.

'Want to know what I did?' he asked. 'I hit him. Sigmar told me he would not save my people, and I hit him. He would not even look me in the eyes as he said it. I hit him in the back of his fat, divine head.' He raised his balled fist, showing it to Yndrasta. '"We must reinforce our allies in Ulgu," Sigmar told me. Bloody-handed Morathi and that black-heart Malerion! Can you believe it? Look what he got for it!' Voyi huffed. 'I struck Sigmar, little as it meant. Then I stole what I thought would save my people and I left.' His eyes flitted to the great axe. 'It wasn't enough. Maybe I am a spoilt brat, huntress. Maybe I wanted too much. Not everyone gets what they deserve. But I hope Sigmar does. And I hope you do, too.'

Yndrasta averted her eyes. 'I did not come for this.'

'No. You came for the Anomia. You won't let me forget it.' He spat. 'At best, you're a fool. At worst, you're more terrible than the things you hunt. Given all this power, and look what you do with it. Bully feeble men in their hiding places. To protect your paltry ego, and your fat god's vainglory. I won't help you. All you'll do is come for me next.'

A screech resounded through the cave from above, distorted by distance and Shyishan geology. The Anomia.

Frustrated, Yndrasta exhaled. There was no more time. 'Voyi–'

A threshing sound drew closer, like a chain hewing through air.

The axe.

Yndrasta dived. The glimmering battle-axe carved through the space where she had just stood. The blazing weapon hurtled into the darkness, then back, severing willow fronds before clanging into Voyi's metal hand.

'I'll not go back,' he growled. 'I'll not face a hypocrite's justice, and I'll not let you deliver it!'

He hurled the axe again. This time Yndrasta had no time to dodge. The weapon smashed into her, exploding against her armour with a volcano's heat.

She flew back. Voyi swept into the wake of his blow. Yndrasta recovered, but fighting him off was like holding back an eruption. Each of his strikes was sheer elemental force, the kind of energy which shattered realms. Pitying him had been a mistake.

Voyi redoubled his efforts, but now Yndrasta was prepared. She found her footing, adjusted her weight. He struck. She dodged. His mighty blows rushed through empty air. Soon his strength flagged. Voyi was old, drained. He could only continue for so much longer. Breathing hard, he withdrew and cocked his shoulder, telegraphing another throw.

Yndrasta's eyes shot to his worldsplitter, so much like Thengavar. Charged with the same energy. Possessed of the same force.

Gritting his teeth, Voyi threw his axe.

Yndrasta, unblinking, caught it.

The look on Voyi's face said much. Yndrasta bowled him to the ground and roared, her spittle stringing across his face. Voyi's pot toppled, dousing the glowing cinders of his fire. Ash plumed where he fell.

Yndrasta raised the axe, her blood boiling over. Pent force travelled up the axis of her body, from her toes to her fingertips, to be unleashed through the weapon's merciless edge. A perfect swing, for a perfect strike, for a *perfect kill*–

Then Voyi howled, arching his back. He flailed beneath Yndrasta's weight, struggling to brush the burning coals out from beneath his spine.

Yndrasta watched with hollow eyes. Recollections of the woman she once was resolved out of the mists of her memory. She remembered taking to the air with her tribe, on the backs of their galloping pegasi. She remembered their great hunts, driving prey towards each other between the mountains of their people. Even then the kill was effortless. Satisfying. Then the realm came apart, in fire and blood, and a daemontide washed against the foothills of those mountains like a deluge. To battle back the daemons and their pagan hordes, Yndrasta united her tribesmen with their old adversaries. Nobody else helped them. Nobody.

Yndrasta blinked. That mortal woman died doing the only thing she knew how: driving her spear into the flank of a daemon king whose shadow darkened horizons. She still remembered howling as she did it, howling as the titanic daemon split her in twain. Not from pain, but *satisfaction*.

It had been so long, but Yndrasta had not changed. Not at all. She enjoyed what she had become. She enjoyed the eternal hunt far more than she had ever loved anything before, even her own people. It was complicated. It was never simple. But whatever Yndrasta had become, she was not this. A senseless killer, enslaved to violence.

She looked at Voyi again and saw him for what he was: a suffering old man, nothing like her.

Betrayer, or betrayed. Did it even matter? Yndrasta could kill him. Tie his head to her belt, and return to Sigmar with something – anything – to make up for the Anomia. She wouldn't even regret it.

She hurled Voyi's worldsplitter. The weapon thudded into the Judgement Willow, quivering in its trunk. Then Yndrasta waded into the dark waters of the Black Pond, preparing to leave.

Voyi scrambled off the coals of his fire, panting. 'Where are you going?'

Yndrasta's eyes bristled. 'To kill the Anomia.'

'You don't know how.'

'Then I shall learn how!' Yndrasta snapped. 'Not all of us have given up on the world, Voyi. Not all of us have given up on ourselves. I don't know what Sigmar did to you, or if the sagas are true. But I know you are broken and I am not. I am a slayer. A monster, too. Fine. But I choose this path. I choose to slay Kragnos and the Anomia and to let you live. And if you think for a moment my choices make me as bad as the things I kill, you are either jaded or a senile fool. And you are wrong, Voyi. So wrong.'

Yndrasta beat her wings, flinging off moisture which had dewed on her pinions. She poised to take flight.

Voyi's face twisted. 'You already defeated it.'

Yndrasta paused, glaring. 'Don't.'

'The Anomia cannot be slain. But it can be frightened, and in that state, bound. If the daemon has revealed its true form, it is vulnerable. You need only walk up and pluck something from it. Sigmar's strength shall protect you.' He chuckled bitterly. 'Take its head, huntress. Your weapon shall be returned, and the Anomia will not take form again.'

Yndrasta's face wrenched up. She could not wrap her mind around it. 'I don't understand.'

'No. It is a paradox. A contradiction, as it is meant to be. Only daemons and fools understand it. We need only accept it.'

Yndrasta's gaze softened. 'Why, Voyi?'

Voyi groaned. He sounded exactly as tired and old as he must be. 'I did not betray Sigmar. I loved him. I loved everything he ever did. But when he told me no...' His voice cracked.

Again, Yndrasta's eyes bristled with some foreign feeling. To look at Voyi felt like looking at something within herself, something naked and ugly and weak.

Voyi's jaw set. 'Perhaps monsters are what we need. Or, if not monsters... then whatever you are. You're better than I was, Yndrasta. And when you dispatch the Anomia, I beg you, return and destroy me yourself. I'll not face him again.'

Yndrasta glanced up, into the leering darkness. Battle called her. When it was done, finding her way back here would be easy. So would ending Voyi's life. It might even be a mercy, in some perverse sense of the word. But a nagging feeling crept in the base of her legs, up her back, into her cold, cracked heart. A kind of irresolute doubt, pulling at the very substance of her. Pity. Or maybe some kinder version of that sentiment.

Yndrasta had never lied to Sigmar before. The God-King trusted her.

Maybe that would make doing it this once easier.

'Rest, Voyi,' Yndrasta said. 'There are no monsters here.'

She beat her wings, hurtling into the darkness in search of nightmares to slay.

YOUR NEXT READ

DOMINION
by Darius Hinks

Witness the destructive forces that are on the rise in the Realm of Beasts first-hand, and see the indomitable defences of Excelsis tested like never before.

For these stories and more, go to **blacklibrary.com**, **games-workshop.com**, Games Workshop and Warhammer stores, all good book stores or visit one of the thousands of independent retailers worldwide, which can be found at **games-workshop.com/storefinder**

Amor Fati

Michael F Haspil

I

Eidolon stood before them in the *Proudheart*'s battle cage unarmed and clad only in a loincloth.

Four more slaves charged. This batch, like the others, held weapons sourced from the Chapter's own armoury. Powerblades and a chainaxe. The largest of the swords merely an initiate's gladius, a *main gauche* for an Astartes warrior. They frothed at the mouth with a mixture of bile, saliva and inchoate rage, fuelled by Fabius' concoction.

By contrast, Eidolon breathed in ragged gasps, not due to exertion, but through frustration and a rage of his own. Subconsciously he raised his hand to his throat. His fingers sought out the raised weal of the suture which circumscribed his neck. His arm convulsed and twitched of its own volition and filled him with revulsion and magnificent pain.

One moment's genuine misunderstanding. Eidolon had not chosen his words with enough care…

* * *

Fulgrim whirled on him, his arm arced back. The anathame glittered in the transcendent light. Eidolon now saw his adored primarch as only enemies did, and he was glorious! The most perfect being he had ever loved.

Combat instinct forced him to move. His hand drew his own blade, brought it up in a doomed attempt to parry the will of a god. Eidolon felt himself knocked across the chamber. He fell on the terrazzo floor, slid, and tumbled, then crashed to a stop.

Strangely he felt no pain.

He tried to regain his footing, but his body didn't respond. He saw Fulgrim turn away from a decapitated figure – sword still firmly in the scabbard.

He blinked in disbelief as the sensations of shock, confusion and betrayal roiled for his attention. Fulgrim grasped him by the hair and spoke, but Eidolon couldn't make out the words. His attention on the mortal realm waned, but instead of finding darkness to greet him, a kaleidoscope of colours met him and something – he struggled to remember – squatted on the edge of his perceptions like a half-forgotten name.

The slaves' attacks returned him to the moment.

He killed the first two without foreplay for the audacity of bringing him from his reverie, then slapped away the third's thrust and caved in its sternum with a punch. He sent the last's body sliding across the marble deck to rest at the base of a stone pillar, amongst the wreckage of mangled battle servitors.

He grew bored. His concentration and purpose for this exercise slipped from him as the experiences of their deaths turned flat and grey and dull. He flipped his once lustrous hair – now stringy and clumped into patchy strands – from out of his view and ran his hand over his face. Frail parchment skin stretched taut over sunken cheeks confirmed the affront to the perfection he had always sought.

Fulgrim's words echoed in his mind. *'The fault lies with Fabius and his imperfect work. Remind me to punish him for making you stupid and ugly.'*

Without Fabius, Eidolon would still be entertained by or entertaining whatever lay beyond the veil… whatever it was he couldn't remember.

'More,' he growled.

Fabius answered him, 'This is a waste and will not achieve what you seek.'

'Can you not still render their bodies and distil their essences for your unguents and libations?'

'I can. But their sentient suffering is lost, and you'll agree that something of the flavour is dampened, resulting in a base and pedestrian death, instead of an experience worthy of my talents,' Fabius said. The great machine known as the chirurgeon clicked and whirred on his back.

'More,' Eidolon repeated.

This next group held little promise save for one. A tall man, powerfully built, bore many scars. Where the other three slaves cowered and averted their eyes, he stared directly at Eidolon and dared match his gaze. The depth of hatred in the man's eyes made Eidolon lick his lips. He wondered what it must be like for this man to have lost everything and be moments from a meaningless death, yet still stand defiant. A warrior.

'Fabius, do not give that one the liquid madness – only the physical stimulants, I want his mind intact.'

Fabius shook his head with apparent regret. 'As you will. Such a specimen might have withstood hours under excruciation. A waste of good suffering.'

Stimulants coursed through the man's body. He bounced on

the balls of his feet and bent to retrieve an Astartes combat knife from the pile of weapons. In his grip it looked like a short sword.

As an afterthought, Eidolon realised the other slaves had started to attack him. Uninspired. Indeed, he had already slain one of them subconsciously, barely registering a threat and dispatching it by rote. The other two attacked, but one fell before he could close with Eidolon, betrayed by his body's frail constitution. Eidolon snapped the other man's neck with a series of blows, all punches after the first redundant, the man already dead on his feet.

The warrior barked debased Low Gothic in Eidolon's direction.

Eidolon taunted him in return. 'I am the one who took everything from you. Kill me and you will have vengeance at least.'

The knife's edge glittered, reflecting the dim and flickering lights surrounding the battle cage as the warrior came at him with a series of feints. This piqued Eidolon's interest. There was skill here, enough to appreciate, enough to garner his fleeting interest.

Eidolon's shoulder spasmed and sent uncoordinated twitches down the length of his arm. It ruined the moment and reminded him of his loathsome imperfections.

Damn Fulgrim.

The attack almost presented a threat. The man had confidence, rage and a grim determination, but for the cocktail of emotions to edge towards completion Eidolon needed to meld it with desperation and despair.

Eidolon's genhanced bulk pirouetted into the air and came down perfectly, nearly behind the warrior, and effortlessly plucked the combat knife from his grip. But only in his mind's eye. Instead, his leg buckled when he tried to leap. He stumbled clumsily and nearly fell, only narrowly avoiding the warrior's knife-edge.

He remembered his primarch's words. *'It is a poor puppeteer who controls you,'* Fulgrim had said, his lip curling in distaste. *'Your walk is ugly and foolish, and you move like a greenskin. It offends me, and I do not wish to see it. Stay behind me until you can perambulate with a measure of grace.'*

Eidolon knew what he had to do. On the warrior's next thrust, he moved just a hair too slowly. He intended for the warrior to cut him, to give him a tantalisingly small taste of victory.

Instead, Eidolon's body betrayed him again.

The man's knife plunged into Eidolon's chest, but even with Fabius' stimms flowing through him, the strike lacked the necessary force to push through the black carapace and Eidolon's fused ribcage. The warrior tried to pull the knife back, but it was firmly lodged in the bone. The man backed away, finally sensing the futility of his actions. A pall of despair drove much of the fire from his eyes. He understood now.

Eidolon screamed in frustration. The Laeran organ in his throat began to warble with the harmonic frequencies to form his sonic scream. He suppressed it.

He remembered the knife in his chest, an instant's diversion, the experience entirely unworthy and unnotable. He twisted the blade free and flexed with the pain of it. He offered it back to the warrior, who spat in defiance. Eidolon tossed the knife at the man's feet, but even that action was clumsy and awkward. Centuries of skilled practice lost. This brought Eidolon a tiny burst of self-pity.

There was luxury in self-pity, but the experience of it was of a mean sort, unworthy for a lord commander of Eidolon's stature. One who'd help slay a demigod and birth a new god in his place.

'I move like a greenskin.' Eidolon repeated his primarch's assessment and let the rage boil over.

Even as the warrior swooped to retrieve the combat knife,

Eidolon was on him. His hand snatched the man's throat, lifted him bodily into the air, and slammed him into the decking. The man's head snapped back from the force of the blow and his skull cracked, spraying blood and brains across the marble.

'More,' Eidolon demanded.

'I think not,' Fabius replied.

Eidolon whirled on the Apothecary. 'You dare defy me openly?'

Fabius barked a laugh, as if to say it hadn't been the first time and it wouldn't be the last, the open challenge in his manner self-evident. 'I only mean to say you will not find what you seek murdering pathetic slaves.'

'And what do I seek?' Eidolon asked.

Fabius didn't answer, prompting him to continue.

Eidolon picked at the scab which had formed from his chest wound and allowed the blood to flow and coagulate once more. 'Lucius was slain by a loyalist, was he not? Were not his circumstances similar to mine? Why is he not afflicted with these maladies?'

Fabius answered, 'He did not suffer a primarch's ire. And he was scarcely dead. It was beneath my talents to restore Lucius. A parlour trick.'

'Your experiments upon my corpse, perfected upon my undeserving brother.'

'Think what you will. But if you understood artistry as much as you pretend to, you would revel in deepest rapture at the miracle I alone have wrought.'

Eidolon grunted, unwilling to concede Fabius' point. His head jerked and sent spasms and agony running down both his arms.

Fabius took on a pensive look and began to pace along the circumference of the battle cage. He spoke to himself, 'Perhaps there may be a way. Yes. It would be interesting in the very least and provide precious data for–'

'What? How? What way?' Eidolon pressed himself against the walls of the battle cage. His fingers entwined in the wire mesh.

'I might be able to reverse the effects and restore you completely to your former glories. I would need the progenoid glands from one of the Legion.'

'Easy enough to acquire.' Eidolon's mind was already sorting through which of his brethren he'd be willing to sacrifice.

'Not so. It would need to be untouched by the Dark Prince's gifts.'

'There's the rub,' Eidolon said. 'Am I to comb and sift through the ashes of Isstvan III?'

'There are others whom you may seek. Secrets from an ancient shame. If they persist...' Lost in his own thoughts, Fabius swept out of the chamber.

Eidolon made to follow the Apothecary, but first moved to the body of the warrior and awkwardly knelt beside the corpse's head. He poked around the ragged edges of the broken skull and fished out a chunk of grey matter and popped it into his mouth, savouring the greasy taste of it. His omophagea gland processed and distilled the man's final memories and emotions so that Eidolon could experience them.

Eidolon savoured the cocktail of sensations. He relished the man's recognition of his doom, but simultaneous refusal to accept defeat. His death wasn't a complete waste; more than a mere *amuse-bouche*.

He threw back his head and roared.

II

It took Fabius nearly a fortnight to recover the secret he'd kept from the Emperor's Children.

When the III Legion had been afflicted by the malady known

as the Blight, Fabius had removed a dozen legionaries from contact with the rest of the Legion, thus preserving an unafflicted control group. Fabius himself had never succumbed, despite close contact with the afflicted, even as his word condemned so many to keep the gene-seed pure. Perhaps he'd used these 'survivors' as his own personal larder. Eidolon wondered what other secrets the Apothecary held close, and whether the Blight had truly been conquered by his ministrations.

Eidolon considered this while he lounged within one of the pleasure suites aboard the *Proudheart*. He felt they were closing on their prey but couldn't be sure. A movement from Kynska's *Maraviglia* played at a near-deafening volume from wall-mounted emitters. The debased music suited Eidolon's current mindset and mood.

They had travelled to Fabius' last known coordinates only to find a recently deserted fortress. Within, they'd discovered six graves, dust-covered armour reverently placed behind crude stone effigies. The group had not been as free of the Blight as Fabius had hoped. What good would tainted gene-seed afford Eidolon?

If there was any chance to restore himself to his former majesty, Eidolon owed it to himself and to the Legion to seek it out. He took a long pull at a hookah primed with the Gift of Bliss, a concoction of the Phoenician himself – meant to open the gates of perception and act as a means of divination.

Eidolon's thoughts turned to Lucius. Lucius, also resurrected, but with none of the afflictions Eidolon suffered. No loss of coordination. No loss of skill. Lucius, the upstart captain, who threatened Eidolon at every opportunity. The next time Lucius attempted to show him up, there should be a reckoning. But only if Eidolon could be whole, or Lucius might beat him.

The ship lurched and the flickering Neverborn attempting to

manifest in the dark corners of the room faded from existence. The *Proudheart* had slipped from the empyrean back into real-space days ahead of schedule.

Eidolon activated the nearest vox-unit. 'What is happening?'

'Lord commander, we have entered realspace. Unknown as to why,' Voidmaster Lyran Tios responded.

Eidolon knew why. He couldn't explain it. He simply understood. His quarry was close.

'There is a world nearby, is there not?'

'Yes, lord commander. But how did you–'

'Do not concern yourself. Ready a Storm Eagle with a squad of Kakophoni. Carnolon Gorrager's squad. I will make planetfall shortly.'

He didn't wait for the reply and strode from the chamber to arm himself.

III

Eidolon allowed his instincts to guide him, and he relayed his orders to the Storm Eagle's pilot. Only he had been blessed with the vision to comprehend their fortuitous drop into realspace from the empyrean. He understood it as the gods' benediction upon his endeavour and their sanction to the restoration of their champion.

The craft flew low over the nightside of a tectonically tortured moon.

'Sensors detecting a structure,' the pilot relayed from the cockpit.

The sensor feed from the troop compartment bathed the squad in an amber glow. The feed upon the static and distortion-filled monitor resolved itself into the Standard Template Construction of a small fortress-monastery.

'There they are,' Eidolon said.

'Who?' the Kakophoni squad champion, Carnolon Gorrager, asked; his speech emerged from his fused vox-grille gurgling with phlegm.

'My quarry.'

'You have told us very little, lord commander. We would perform better–'

Eidolon cut him off. 'My orders alone should suffice, no?'

Gorrager nodded grudgingly. The rest of his squad fidgeted in place, and Eidolon appreciated their eagerness to drink in new sensations.

Eidolon smiled at Gorrager and gave in a bit. 'They are loyalists, Gorrager. Nothing more. Loyalist scum who may possess something I... *we*... need. Pilot, put us down in that ravine.'

The Storm Eagle had scarcely alighted on the moon's surface when Eidolon bounded down the exit ramp, his warhammer resting on his shoulder. The Kakophoni moved behind him and immediately spread out in an echelon formation suitable for a small unit on patrol.

They struck out in the direction of the fortress-monastery. The ravine, a shallow affair from the air, proved to be a deep rent in the moon's surface. Geometric basalt columns stretched skyward – tubes from a monstrous pipe organ, near-vertical walls which cut off what little ambient light reached the floor and left behind large patches of Stygian gloom. Sulphurous mists choked the hexagon-patterned ground masking occasional bottomless fissures, which glowed faintly orange from a source deep below. Eidolon's footsteps scraped along the ground and disturbed crystalline shards which uttered vaguely resonant tones as they were kicked away or crushed underfoot.

Gorrager scanned the walls of the ravine, the tension in his body evident in his every movement. 'They will have detected us, lord commander. You should be on your guard.'

Not *we.*

Suspicion lurked at the edge of Eidolon's thoughts. Gorrager's loyalties within the III Legion might lie elsewhere, but he wouldn't dare act against Eidolon in the open.

Would he?

Truth be told, Eidolon had selected such a small escort because he wanted to hold his secrets close. Trust was in short supply and he needed persons the Legion would not miss if it came down to it. Had he misjudged? He might have faced down the entire squad before his ordeal. Could he survive such a combat with his body as clumsy and unresponsive as it was?

Eidolon sucked at the volcanic fumes and relished the way they grated and scraped along his throat. 'I should hope our erstwhile brothers would not have grown so slovenly that they could miss a Storm Eagle overflying them. They may not know who we are. They may think us survivors of Isstvan V, or other lost brothers. They will send out a patrol to investigate. And if the gods are good, the one we seek will be among them. You see, we seek a fellow legionary of the Third. One who isn't as… *enlightened* as we've become, but who nevertheless possesses an item of great value. Which *I* require. Rest assured you will be well rewarded.'

Gorrager barely grunted in acknowledgement. There was a warbling tone to his response, indicating his preparedness to let loose with the sonic weaponry the Kakophoni were known for.

Ahead, a small shower of rocks fell from a concealed position. A man-made sound, unmistakable as anything else. But it was also such that it hadn't been made in error. The Kakophoni dispersed and sought sparse cover. Eidolon didn't move. Without his helmet, he had no auto-senses to highlight the potential targets ahead. He found he didn't need them. He *knew* where they were and could picture them in his mind's eye as surely as if he'd seen them under the brightest sky.

A clear voice spoke out through the mist. 'Far enough, traitors.'

Eidolon responded louder than he normally would, his voice projected theatrically for the benefit of his unseen audience. The Laeran organ in his larynx added a buzzing substratum to his words and gave the echoes an eldritch quality. 'Long have we sought each other. Speak.'

'I am the last of the Third Legion,' the voice said matter-of-factly.

'Not so. We are of the Third. You speak with Lord Commander Eidolon. Come forth so that we may be reunited, brother.'

'You do not fear the Blight?' the voice said. 'The Apothecary, Fabius, told us not to return to the Legion's bosom, for fear that we might be corrupted. But it was already too late.'

'The Blight no longer troubles us. We have a cure if you are afflicted.' Inwardly, Eidolon prayed his quarry wasn't. 'We have come so very far since your time amongst us. We have such wondrous sights to show you. Show yourself,' Eidolon commanded and raised a palsied finger to point directly at the voice's position as if to demonstrate there was no more use in hiding.

The voice sighed, and Eidolon could hear a measure of anguish in its tone even across the distance. 'Ah, I see you clearly now. It is as I was told. I see you as the debased malformities you have become. Would that my eyes had been plucked from my skull rather than see this blasphemy that has befallen the Legion.'

'No more subterfuge, come forth. It is better this way, is it not? Know that I would pluck from you more than your simple eyes. Though you still claim to see, you are blind to the truth… to reality. I would try to show you, but alas, I fear I am here for your martyrdom.'

Fifty metres ahead, a bulky silhouette stood from the concealment of a jagged basalt outcrop and resolved itself in the swirling mist.

'You stand among abominations, perversions of our true and

noble form crafted in the image of the Emperor and granted the honour of bearing His mark, as no other Legion could. Know this, lord commander, I am Sergeant Avram Rakomon. This day, I take vengeance upon you for your treachery, betrayal and desecration of all our Legion holds dear. You will meet your end by my hand.'

Eidolon ran his tongue against his teeth and lips. He savoured the bitter mineral-laced atmosphere and the scorn projected in the sergeant's words. 'Well met, Rakomon. Let us end this.'

Eidolon hefted his hammer in his right hand and gripped the shaft near the head, the better to run with it. He drew his archeotech pistol and, with an elated cry, charged. Gorrager called out from behind him, 'Wait!' Eidolon gave him no heed. He glanced briefly over his shoulder to note that the Kakophoni followed, then returned the full measure of his attention upon his prey.

The dim light of their surroundings blossomed into staccato flashes of light as the loyalists executed their ambush and mass-reactive shells detonated on the Kakophoni's armour. Their sonic weaponry answered with blasts of coherent sound powerful enough to smash ceramite, rend flesh and break bone – shattering the rock around them and sending stony shrapnel in every direction.

But the loyalists had the advantage.

Eidolon did the only thing he could and ran through the ambush to get out of the kill-zone. He caught glimpses of Iron Hands and Salamanders. Visibility was poor enough even with auto-senses; the loyalists wouldn't dare fire for fear of hitting one of their own. Eidolon had no such concern. He'd considered his Kakophoni as dead men the instant they'd boarded the Storm Eagle.

Eidolon broke from the mist nearly on top of an Iron Hands

legionary. They both stood startled at one another for the briefest instant, then reacted simultaneously. The Iron Hands Space Marine brought his bolter to bear on Eidolon, while Eidolon switched his grip on the hammer. At that moment, his fingers failed him, and he nearly dropped it. Instead, he let his pistol hang by its restraint lanyard and brought his other hand to steady the hammer.

He was too clumsy and too late.

The other Space Marine's bolter barked even as Eidolon swung. By providence or by chance, the shell deflected from Eidolon's pauldron and detonated harmlessly against nearby stone. Eidolon's swing ended in a thunderclap as the energised hammer's head stove in the Iron Hands legionary's chest and smashed his body against the ravine wall. Eidolon raised the hammer for a *coup de grâce,* but the Space Marine had been pulverised.

Eidolon stood, slack-jawed at the result. He'd struck in the heat of the moment, with a practised strike he'd executed perhaps thousands of times. Never with such a result. Eidolon had only seen one other deal such a blow. And that being had been a primarch.

He scanned for the next target and saw one of the Kakophoni drop as a bolter round struck him through the eye-lens. The mass-reactive shell blew out the back of the Space Marine's skull and helmet.

The Kakophoni's sonic weapons reached a maddening crescendo. The echoes of their braying blasts melded with the discordant notes from the perverted instruments to unleash an orgy of ruinous sound. The pain, even to Eidolon's appreciative ears, was extreme. A delightful experience, the crudeness of which held a sort of majesty of its own. Eidolon relished it. Loyalist legionaries fell before them, organs and armour ruptured simultaneously, leaving their owners to grovel and die in tortured agony. Even Adeptus Astartes physiology could not recover from wounds such as these.

The loyalists fell back, regrouped, and re-engaged. A blast from a plasma weapon struck one of the Kakophoni nearest Eidolon. The legionary's torso boiled away into superheated gas. The Salamander who'd fired turned his attention to Eidolon and prepared to fire again.

There was no time to strike with his hammer and his pistol bounced freely on its lanyard as he ran. Even as his left hand clumsily grasped for the pistol, Eidolon focused his sonic shriek on the warrior before him. The Salamander reacted instinctively and sought to shield himself with his plasma gun. It was the last thing he would ever do. Eidolon's Laeran scream unbalanced something deep within the weapon and it detonated like a grenade, leaving the warrior's legs to topple independently onto the ground.

There was no more incoming fire and the riot of noise from the Kakophoni died down to mere echoes.

Eidolon took stock of the situation. The loyalists had been defeated and if any were left, they were in retreat. But the battle could not have gone unnoticed, and reinforcements would be inbound from the fortress. He grasped his pistol, and movement to his periphery made him bring it to bear. He lowered it when he saw Gorrager had survived.

'Do you see the member of the Third?' he asked Gorrager, desperation tingeing his question despite himself.

'The Kakophoni are dead,' Gorrager answered with disbelief in his tone.

'Not the Kakophoni, you fool. That loyalist sergeant we spoke with. Rakomon,' Eidolon corrected.

Gorrager turned on him, disrespect in his every word. 'He was wounded and fled. What do I care what became of him? Let him rot.'

'I cannot. He is the entire reason for all this,' Eidolon said.

'Yet you still won't tell me why. Only your order should suffice. You and your pride have doomed this mission.'

Eidolon closed the distance to Gorrager in an instant, and his arm moved nearly of its own volition. Before he even realised it, he'd backhanded Gorrager several metres off the ground. The Kakophoni champion crashed down and skidded away from him.

'You dare question me?' Eidolon screamed, his altered larynx doubling his words and preparing to unleash another shriek.

'Come to your senses, lord commander. Your hubris has brought this about.'

Eidolon closed the distance casually, rage deafening him to reason. 'You are mistaken, Gorrager. Hubris only applies to those not up to the task.'

Gorrager tried to climb to his feet and bring his sonic weapon to bear. 'Lucius was right about you.'

Anger flared throughout Eidolon's entire being at the swordsman's name. 'Lucius? You are in league with him?'

Gorrager had time to say 'No–' before Eidolon's hammer made a ruin of his head and his body toppled back to the ground. Elation mingled with regret. Eidolon hadn't meant to kill him, only punish him for his insubordination. Fabius would hold no salvation for Gorrager.

Was this how Fulgrim felt?

Part of Eidolon chided himself for comparing himself to his primarch, but then another portion rebelled. After all, why shouldn't he? He marvelled at the strength he'd displayed when he struck Gorrager. A gift from the Dark Prince. If Fulgrim could ascend to daemonhood, could not Eidolon ascend above his station as well?

Still, he needed to return to the task at hand. He moved up the ravine looking for any sign of the sergeant, Rakomon. Gorrager had said he'd been injured, and Eidolon used his heightened senses to search. As he cleared the ambush site, he flicked his tongue across his teeth and delighted in the scent of fresh Astartes blood. He moved quickly to find the trail, and it seemed to him that the blood nearly fluoresced under the vented fog which suffused the moon's surface.

All too quickly, the trail abated as the sergeant's transhuman physiology began to heal the wound. But it was too late for him. Eidolon spotted him hobbling not thirty metres away.

'You flee in the face of a foe? Only you and I remain, brother. Here stands your chance to avenge all your wrongs. I thought I would meet my end through your hands. Or were those mere words?' Eidolon taunted.

Rakomon turned deliberately. The sword's blade in his hand crackled with energy and illuminated the hatred in his features as he swung it before him in a perfunctory salute.

'You will fall this day, *lord commander.*' Rakomon spoke the title with a mockery of the respect it deserved.

Champions to their cause, the two Space Marines sprinted towards one another heedless of the stone shards skittering and punctuating each footstep with musical tones.

Each an avatar of the III Legion.

One of the past.

One of the future.

Rakomon closed the final steps with a flurry of calculated blows that would easily fell a lesser combatant. He was no Lucius in his swordplay, but the warrior was not without skill. Yet, Eidolon caught or parried each strike deftly on the head of his hammer. The competing energy fields combined with the echoes of the combat and the crystalline harmonics of the stone underfoot to create a series of unique disharmonies that made Eidolon's blood sing within him as accompaniment.

A laugh burbled forth from his chest, and on Rakomon's next strike, Eidolon locked the blade with the back side of his hammer and pulled the sergeant into a tight *corps-a-corps.*

'Do you hear it? Is this not how it was meant to be, brother?' Eidolon shouted.

Rakomon grunted with effort, brought his knee up and kicked at Eidolon's chest. Though Eidolon stood unmoving, the blow presented Rakomon with the leverage he needed to break free. The loyalist fell to his back, rolled, and recovered his footing by launching a renewed attack. Eidolon repelled it easily. He wasn't moving any faster; it was as if he'd fought this combat before. As if every move had been rehearsed a hundred times. Rakomon screamed in frustration, but his strikes never abated.

Eidolon stopped the latest blow. 'You really are trying, aren't you? How delightfully tragic.'

In truth, Eidolon was already losing interest, the experience growing stale.

'Apologies, brother,' he said, 'but you have something I need.'

Rakomon started to respond with his next strike, but Eidolon used it to issue a devastating riposte. The hammer caught Rakomon full in the chest with the force of a meteor impact and silenced him forever. The sergeant's body blasted backwards and crashed to the ground, a great rent apparent in the armour's chestplate, sundering the Emperor's aquila in two.

Eidolon prised his fingers into the crack and pulled. In a feat of incredible power, he broke the compromised chestplate apart. Then, unconcerned with other damage he might cause to himself or to the body, he dug his fingers into the sergeant's flesh, through the black carapace, and punched the body until he cracked through the fused ribcage. He recognised the valuable progenoid glands, the pure gene-seed, and, unbothered by the gore and viscera coating his hands, reached into the sergeant's chest cavity and tore them away. He shouted in triumph just as distant engines approached.

Loyalist reinforcements.

Eidolon took one last look at Sergeant Rakomon and presented him with a scornful salute. But in that act, he saw the sergeant not even as a fellow legionary, but as a puny, ruined, pathetic thing completely unworthy of his attention.

He turned and bounded towards the Storm Eagle. His thoughts returned to the feats which had led him to this point. How had he known where to find his prize? He'd trusted his instincts. His senses were preternaturally honed beyond anything they'd been before. The strength he'd exhibited and not known he was capable of...

These were gifts from the gods.

No, not gifts. Boons, perhaps, for the gods would always want their payment. And if he let Fabius return him to his previous state, then that would be to spit upon the Dark Prince and whatever destiny he had planned for Eidolon. And he was destined for momentous events. Why else was he alive if not for greatness? Perhaps Fabius knew this, and it was his plan to rip Eidolon from his glorious destiny and return him to a mewling, pathetic existence shared by much of the Legion.

Mediocrity was not to be his lot. Fulgrim had now ascended and would no longer concern himself with the mundane affairs of the Legion. Yet the III would need leadership and guidance, and who better than Eidolon to wear that mantle?

As the Storm Eagle came into view, Eidolon suffered a final measure of clarity. All his remembered existence, he had sought perfection in all things – in warfare, strategy, tactics; in martial arts; in arts of a different sort. The Dark Prince had unveiled the mysteries of experience only the most elevated and debauched could truly appreciate. Then Eidolon had become soul-severed, and now perfection in his most intimate possession, his own body, was forever lost to him – constantly in blissful agony, reminded eternally of his shame as his body refused to obey his mind.

In its own way, it was a perfect torment, tailor-made for the rest of his existence.

He could fathom no more ideal torture for himself. He could embrace it, and his new gifts, and rise with no limit to his power. Or he could reject it and be restored to his previous mundane perfection. He appreciated the subtle majesty of it and at once understood, adored and lamented his fate. His curse was also a boon. An insignificant price to pay for his new-found abilities. The Dark Prince was wise beyond measure. It was to be an eternal blessing paid for by a never-ending agony.

He glared at the precious organ in his hand and crushed it.

Delicious.

YOUR NEXT READ

HORUS RISING
by Dan Abnett

His dream for humanity accomplished, Emperor hands over the reins of power to his Warmaster, Horus, and heads back to Terra. But will such incredible power corrupt Horus?

The Vintage

David Annandale

'You will command Fovos Keep.'

Ullior Arkhant looked up at Venthor Warfire, and wished he had misheard. The Lord-Celestant of the Anvils of the Heldenhammer looked back at him, waiting for a response.

They were on the roof of the keep's central tower. The circular rampart gave a commanding view of the bleak lands surrounding Fovos. Once, this had been an agricultural region, but the fields had been swept clear of topsoil many years before, and were now nothing but an expanse of black, wind-blown stone. The keep's storerooms were large, and it could withstand a siege for a long time on what was in them. To replenish them, though, Fovos depended on caravans reaching it from the distant free cities of Veilgard and Port Sorrow. The routes from anywhere to Fovos were long and uninviting, and the only strategic importance it held was that Venthor's chamber of the Anvils of the Heldenhammer had come this way in their campaign to free more settlements in Shyish. Their path could just as easily have taken them elsewhere, and Fovos would have remained empty, a shell to be worn down by the centuries and elements. Its position as a point of connection between Veilgard and Port Sorrow was tenuous.

The challenges the keep faced were of concern to Ullior. They were not why Venthor's words filled him with dread.

In all directions, the stony emptiness stretched for as far as Ullior could see. Coreward, in the far distance, the dark hills rose from the plain. Just barely visible on the highest hill, so far away that it appeared thin as a hair, was the source of Ullior's dread. The tower was shaped like a twisted claw. Its name was Penumbrial. Ullior felt its presence even when he was not looking in its direction. He had stared at the crooked tower a lot since arriving at Fovos. He had been eager for the campaign to move on. He had not expected he would have to stay.

'You have proven yourself in battle many times over,' Venthor continued. 'Fovos must be held, and it is clear to me that under your command, it will be. Be proud of your new post, Ullior Arkhant. You have done much to earn it.'

'Wouldn't I be more useful fighting at your side, Lord-Celestant?' Ullior asked. 'There are hard battles awaiting us Edgeward.'

'There are indeed. But it is important, too, to hold the ground we have captured. That is why your skills are needed here.'

'The walls of Fovos are strong and high,' said Ullior. And they were, especially now that they had been repaired and reinforced. The rings of walls were like cliffs, each wall taller and thicker than the last, and it seemed to Ullior that the walls were only there to protect the stores, and the stores were there only to ensure the protection of the walls. Fortification was the sole purpose of the Fovos Keep's existence.

'The walls are only as good as their defenders,' said Venthor. 'You are the true strength of Fovos Keep.'

Ullior bowed his head in humility. There would be no changing the Lord-Celestant's mind. But it was torture to think that the Anvils of the Heldenhammer would leave him behind, after he had been part of their battles in Shyish for so many years. And it was a worse torture to think that they were leaving him *here.*

'Fovos Keep was your home, was it not?' Venthor asked.

'I was born in the village nearby.'

Venthor looked out at the vista of nothingness. 'What village?'

'It's gone now,' said Ullior. 'All the villages that surrounded the keep are gone.' They had left no trace of themselves, no sign that they had ever existed. 'I can't even remember its name.'

Involuntarily, he turned his gaze to Penumbrial.

But I can remember what happened to it.

Ullior was a child when *she* came for his village. How old had he been? He didn't know. Old enough to walk, too young to work in the fields. His only memory of what had been his home was the day of its death.

He remembered walking down the dusty lane that was the closest the village had to a road. He was carrying a few stalks of wheat, pretending to help with the harvest. It was hot, the rays of Hysh baking the back of his neck. Then a wind suddenly blew cold from Coreward. It snatched the stalks from his grasp, and made Ullior look up. Dark clouds scudded overhead, blotting out the sight of Hysh. They fanned out like a grasping hand, and the hand was reaching out from Penumbrial.

Now a new, deeper stain came from the tower, a darkness of wings beneath the clouds, coming straight for the village. They came fast, flying on the winds of nightmare, and even before they arrived, Ullior was surrounded by people running and screaming in panic.

Ullior ran too. Weeping in terror, he ran for his home, the

wood and packed-earth hut that he lived in with his parents. Everyone around left him behind in their flight. He couldn't keep up. His parents were still in the fields. They were too far away for help.

He never saw what happened to them, though his dreams would show him their fate many, many times, in all its terrible variations.

The cloud of wings descended on the village as he neared the hut. Night had come from the tower of Penumbrial, a night of vampires, and they fell on the people with snarls of delighted hunger.

Ullior was almost at the doorway to the hut when a monster flew through the walls. It was huge, a thing of muscle and fangs. The adult Ullior, the warrior, would know the horror as a Vargheist. The child Ullior saw only an embodiment of the monstrous flying mere feet over his head while his home exploded. Roof and walls flew apart, then collapsed, falling towards Ullior. In his memory, the wreckage fell slowly, gently and gradually as feathers, the sight holding him fast, denying his escape. The hand of fate shaped the fall, and the hut came down over Ullior, but not on top of him. The wooden beams tented as they came down, forming a dark shelter over his crouching form.

He shivered and wept, but he was unharmed. When the groaning of the ruin subsided, the screams from beyond it forced him to open his eyes and peer through the gaps between the splintered timbers.

He witnessed the slaughter of everyone he knew. The vampires swept through the village like a swarm of locusts. Winged horrors snatched their prey into the air, fed, and then dropped the twitching, bleeding bodies. Cloaked predators on foot sprinted from home to home, fast as the wind that had brought them. The screams that came from inside the huts were brief, but agonised. Many of the victims were not killed outright. They were left in the road, helpless and terrified. They were left there by the vampires as offerings to their mistress.

And then *she* arrived. Anasta Malkorion, the Countess of Dread, strode up the road, her gait both leisurely and majestic. Her high ribbed collar was in the shape of a claw made of blood and terror. It framed her hairless skull. Her flesh was paler than fear, a white so deathly it was tinged with grey and green. Her ratlike fangs protruded from her thin lips. Though she took her time to walk, her head flicked back and forth with short, sudden movements as she caught one scent, and then another. She carried a long sword in one hand. With the other, she cradled a familiar, both feline and rodent, and as hairless as she.

Malkorion walked up slowly to each of her victims. She sniffed them as she drew near, and her familiar yowled in excitement. Ullior watched her come up to a man whose leg was broken. She gutted him with a flick of the sword. His scream became a choking hiss as he spilled himself onto the ground. She left him there to bleed and writhe his last, and took a few steps across the road to another man who was staring in horror at what she had done. Malkorion sheathed her sword and picked up the man with one hand as easily as Ullior had been holding the wheat stalks. She held the man's face close to hers, and for several long seconds did nothing. The man shrieked, struggling uselessly in her grip. She held him out at arm's length so he could see the atrocities around them, and then, when he was sobbing in terror of what was going to befall him, she yanked him close again and bit out his throat. She drank his blood greedily, then threw him down. He wasn't quite dead yet, and his painful end served to increase terror in the road even more.

Malkorion moved on, drawing closer to Ullior's refuge. She killed more with her blade, and fed on the blood of witnesses.

She sent her familiar scurrying into homes, where it found the people in hiding and chased them out with angry shrieks to become part of the countess' ritual of fear and death. Always, Malkorion took her time, savouring each cruelty.

Closer. Closer. Malkorion was only a few yards away from the ruined hut. Ullior was too frightened to scream. He was frozen with dread. The worst moment of all was closing in on him. There was nothing he could do. No one could save him. He didn't fully understand what was happening, except that he was experiencing the most terrible nightmare he had ever had, and that he was wide awake.

Malkorion paused. She was just on the other side of the fallen beams. If she bent down, she would see Ullior, and she was close enough to reach inside and pull him out. His mouth was straining open in a silent scream.

Malkorion moved on.

Ullior closed his eyes. He didn't want to see any more. He covered his ears, but he could not blot out the cries of the murdered. The butchering went on forever, the sounds wet and heavy, a world of horror holding him tighter and tighter in a crushing embrace. But then, at last, the screams and the feeding subsided. Gradually, the roar of fires burning through the village ceased too. Ullior shivered and wept for hours, the silence no comfort, because his parents did not come for him. No one came. He was alone.

It was evening when he dared to move. He pushed at the wreckage, scared he might be trapped, but one of the beams fell at his touch, opening a way out for him. He crawled out from the ruin of his home. He stood up, turning around slowly, looking for someone, for anyone.

The village was dead. He was surrounded by bodies, already being picked over by crows. Smoke rolled over the blackened ruins of huts. There was nothing left here.

He had no one, and nowhere to go.

Ullior walked away from the smouldering village. He headed Edgeward on instinct, away from the tower of the Countess of Dread. He kept stopping, dropping to the ground and staring up at the sky, expecting one of her monsters to descend upon him and carry him away. The clouds lowered at him, the evening brooded, and night came with even darker thoughts.

Nothing came for him.

Ullior's coherent memories of the day came to an end there. He knew that he'd walked through the night, and at some point, he'd encountered the survivors of other slaughtered villages. They were the ones who carried him to Fovos Keep, where he at last found refuge.

Refuge of a kind. He found sanctuary for his body, not for his soul. In it now, and never to leave, was a dread that Anasta Malkorion would come for him sooner or later. She did come for him in his nightmares. She awaited him in his sleep every night of every year as he grew older. When he came of age, he fought the nightmares by honing his ferocity as a warrior. By then, he had wandered far from Fovos, which itself had long been abandoned. When his path crossed that of the Anvils of the Heldenhammer, he saw in them the hope to banish his dread. He beheld the glory of their prowess in battle. Even more importantly, he saw how they died. There was no corpse left behind, languishing in abject gore. Instead, there was the lightning of Sigmar, the ascendance from Shyish and, as Ullior later learned, the eventual return. He heard how Lord-Celestant Venthor had fallen before the gates of Angaria, and yet here he was, leading his chamber again in a march to free the people of Shyish from the terror of the daemons and the tyranny of Nagash.

To be a Stormcast Eternal was to be free of dread. Ullior saw that from the moment he was in their presence. From then on, in all the years that he was one of their mortal followers, he had one goal that was supreme among all others. Even greater than his commitment to the people of Shyish was his need to become one of the Anvils.

Then, he would be free of dread. Then, he would banish Anasta Malkorion from his dreams.

Now, Lord-Celestant Venthor was going to leave him, and make him stay within sight of Penumbrial. The distant shape of the tower scratched at his eye, and at his courage. Nothing had issued from Penumbrial in all the time they had been in this region of Shyish. Malkorion had not challenged the Anvils of the Heldenhammer. There was not even a sign that she still resided in the tower, as if her home were now only in Ullior's dreams.

'If it must fall to me to defend and hold Fovos Keep, then that is what I vow to do,' Ullior said. He would not shirk his duty. But he would make one last attempt to be granted that which would release him from his dread. 'But my prayer is that I am destined to fight forever at your side, Lord-Celestant.' He hesitated, and then, because he was desperate, he said what he had never put into words before. 'Grant that my fate is to become one of your number.' To his humiliation, his voice shook.

'That is not for me to grant,' Venthor said, stern but not unkind. 'That is Sigmar's blessing alone.' He said *blessing* as if it were not truly the correct word.

Ullior bowed his head, face burning in shame. *I had to ask, though. I had to try. You don't understand what you're doing to me.* All the words he could not speak without losing what honour he had left.

The Anvils of the Heldenhammer departed in the late afternoon. Ullior stood at the head of his troops. As this was now their permanent station, they had been newly named the Freeguild Wallguard of Fovos Keep. Their ranks stood to attention as the Anvils marched between them and out of the gates. When Venthor, mounted on his Dracoth, passed by, Ullior thought the look he gave him had a touch of pity.

It gave him no comfort. His dread only increased.

Ullior climbed the steps to the ramparts of the outer wall and watched the column of the Anvils of the Heldenhammer diminish Edgeward until it vanished. Then he turned to address the gathered Wallguard in the courtyard below.

'Comrades of the Freeguild,' he said, 'from this day forward, Fovos will be the most vigilant keep in Shyish. Our watch will never sleep. Through the Anvils of the Heldenhammer, Sigmar has entrusted us to guard this land, and so we shall. Our wars have proven our mettle. Now we will show that what has been captured can be held, and held forever!'

Cheers answered him, and he saw in the faces of the Wallguard the mirror of his own determination. He also saw signs of relief, of reassurance. He had never spoken to anyone of his fears. Were they feeling the dread of Penumbrial too?

He hoped not. Vigilance was necessary for survival, but if the dread was widespread, despite the silence of the tower, then what chance did they have?

Don't think like that. You can't afford to think like that.

Odeeya Bathas, his second-in-command, approached from the other end of the battlement. 'What are your standing orders, captain?' she asked. There was no fear in her wind-leathered features. She had campaigned across leagues and leagues of hard-fought battlefields, and now she was ready to be a sentinel. Her steadiness brought Ullior the stability he needed.

'The emptiness around us must not lull us,' Ullior said. He pointed to Penumbrial. 'The enemy is always before us. The threat will not end until that tower falls.' *If then.* 'Until such a day, Fovos Keep is at maximum alert. And the watch is doubled at night.'

'It shall be done,' said Odeeya.

'The first watch of each night will be mine.'

So, as time passed, was the last one. Ullior found that sleep at night was impossible. After the first watch, in his quarters at the top of the central tower, he lay in bed with his eyes wide open, waiting for the sounds of attack and slaughter. So he would rise again, and stand guard watching Coreward, and not even think about rest until he saw the dawn.

He did try to snatch a few hours of sleep during the day, but the thought of the coming night kept him awake then too. The line between dread and duty vanished. A slave to both, he pushed himself until his endurance began to crack. He felt the wall of exhaustion looming over him. He thought he could hold it from falling onto him a while longer. He thought he was doing well in concealing his strain.

He discovered he was wrong when Odeeya spoke to him, a few weeks after the Anvils of the Heldenhammer had departed. She came up to him late in the afternoon. He was on the walls again, finding some peace in walking them during the day, when he could let himself spend more time on the Edgeward battlement, facing away from Penumbrial.

'Captain,' she said, 'you must sleep.'

'I do,' he said.

'I know that you don't. We all do. You are too present. There are whispers in the ranks. Your guards are wondering what you are doing to yourself. So am I.'

Ullior sighed. 'I apologise. We have been comrades too long for me to lie to you.'

'You have to rest. You are pushing yourself too hard, and will be of no use to anyone.'

'I know,' he admitted.

'Don't you trust us?'

He started. 'Of course I do,' he said.

'Then prove it. Let us do what we are here to do. Let us be vigilant, and stop trying to be vigilant in our place.'

'Yes,' said Ullior. 'Yes,' he said again, with feeling. He felt a wave of shame for having acted as if he doubted the resolution and skill of his guards. After the shame, but needing it to break the dam of his obsession, came relief. For the first time since Venthor had decreed his fate, Ullior understood, and believed, that he wasn't alone.

He thought that he could, at last, sleep.

Storm clouds rolled in that evening, hastening the coming of night, and he welcomed the dark. He knew the dread would come again, but not this night. Ullior vowed he would make it to the morning without giving in to the need to take the watch. If he succeeded, that would be a true victory over the dread. When it returned, it would be weakened. That would be, for him, a triumph worthy of song.

He ate with his fellow guards, and he was cheerful. When he retired to his quarters, the storm broke. It was ferocious, thunder hammering the sky every few seconds, and the rain fell in dark sheets. Ullior looked out Coreward from his window. He couldn't see Penumbrial. It was hidden by the darkness of the night and rain.

Ullior felt his shoulders sag, tension falling from them. *I can't see you,* he told the tower. *And you can't see me.* It was an irrational thought, but it felt true.

The wind gusted, driving the rain into his face. He let it sting and refresh him. Then he closed the shutters. He fell into bed. He listened to the thunder, and to the rain rattling against the windows. The storm embraced him, and he slept.

* * *

Ullior woke, gasping. The nightmare receded from his memory in an instant, but its cold fist still clutched at his heart. The dread was back, worse than ever. The storm still raged, thunder rolling like a rockslide above the keep, the rain sweeping down in roars. But beneath the clamour of the gale, he sensed a silence.

Ullior leapt out of bed and dressed for battle. When he called for an attendant, there was no answer, and the underlying silence grew thicker. Sword in hand, he opened the door to his chamber.

There were no guards in the hall. Ullior called out again, his voice loud and lonely between peals of thunder.

Nothing. No one.

He ran down the short hall to the stairs that spiralled down from the peak of the tower. A dozen steps down, he found the first of the bodies. The guard lay with his head tilted at a right angle, a jagged shard of bone protruding from the bloodless wound.

'Vampires!' Ullior shouted, trying again to raise the alarm. 'We are under attack! There are vampires in the keep!'

The silence beneath the storm smiled at him, and the dread squeezed his chest so hard, he almost vomited.

He ran down the stairs, growing dizzy with terrible anticipation, and raced out onto the ramparts of the keep's highest, innermost wall. Sheet lightning illuminated the slaughter. There were corpses everywhere, some drained of blood, some lying in pools of their gore, the dark liquid mixing with the deep pools of the rain. The deaths had all been violent. The bodies were contorted, the wounds savage. Arms and heads had been scattered across the battlements like the leaves of autumn. One of the heads belonged to Odeeya Bathas. Her face was frozen in desperate anger.

The thunder held its breath. The silence curled around Ullior. He was alone. The terror of his youth, fresh with resurrection, raced through his blood and pierced his heart.

'Are you a child once again?' said a voice dry as a rat's claw.

Ullior turned around, and saw his dread made flesh. Anasta Malkorion was there, not twenty feet away, her sword in the chest of a corpse, her familiar perched on her shoulder and eyeing Ullior with its head cocked. Above, on the battlements of the tower, monsters perched with folded wings.

Malkorion sheathed the sword. She scratched the chin of her familiar and walked towards Ullior. He tightened his grip on his sword, and braced himself for what he had to do.

'Ullior Arkhant,' the vampire said. 'I have waited many years for this moment.'

So had Ullior, for a lifetime of fear. '*No!*' he screamed, and with the desperation born of forty years of nightmares, he charged. As he closed in, he thrust his blade at her throat. With a casual gesture, as if brushing off a fly, she batted the sword from his hand and knocked him to the ground. She stepped on his chest, holding him flat, and leant over him. The hairless skull and its taut, deathly flesh had followed him through his dreams all his life, and now it had caught up to him.

He had lived with his fear of her for so long, it did not seem strange, at first, that she spoke his name. *She never saw me,* he thought now. *How does she know? She never saw me!*

Malkorion grinned. Her teeth glinted in the flash of lightning. 'Yes,' she said. 'I know your name. I know your life. I have watched you grow. I watched the child crawl from the wreckage of his home, and look upon the massacre of everyone he knew. I saw him marked forever by the scene I had designed. I watched the child become the warrior who fought alongside the Anvils of the Heldenhammer, who reaped glory on the battlefield despite the dread in his blood, and who returned at last to Fovos Keep, within the shadow of Penumbrial. I have been close to you more than once, gauging how your blood has matured.'

She paused, and Ullior squirmed, trying to escape the boot that pinned him to the sodden flagstones.

Malkorion laughed. 'Do you think you can escape me? Did you think you *had* escaped me? Did you think your survival that day was an accident of chance?'

Ullior froze. The memory of the worst day of his life rose before him again, and began to take on a different cast. It became darker with every word Malkorion uttered.

'I attacked your village for a special purpose,' said the vampire. 'It was part of a cultivation, the preparation of a very refined vintage of blood. The cultivation required a single survivor. I chose you. For two score years, your dread has grown. A lifetime of dread has matured in your blood, and it is time to decant you.'

She straightened, and removed her foot from his chest. Ullior flipped onto his stomach and clawed at the stones, scrabbling away. A hand, cold and clawed, grabbed him by the neck and hoisted him into the air. His feet kicked fruitlessly.

'Good,' said Malkorion. 'Good.' She turned him around. She examined him closely, brought him close to her face and sniffed. 'Ah,' she said. 'Yes. Yes, it is time.'

With a flick of a claw, she sliced open his throat. His blood jetted out into the night. He started to choke, but Malkorion sank the fingers that gripped him deeper into his flesh, and the pain kept him conscious. She sniffed the air again, and nodded in satisfaction. She dipped a finger into his wound and licked the blood from it.

Ullior tried to scream. He could not. The scream stayed trapped inside his mind. He was screaming because all his nightmares had been preparing him for this. They had been part of his cultivation. He was screaming at the lie of his life, and at the horror of its truth. And he was screaming in dread, because even though he knew he was dying, the worst had not yet happened.

Malkorion snapped her head forward like a viper. She sank her teeth into Ullior's neck, and she savoured his vintage.

She savoured him for a very long time.

YOUR NEXT READ

GOTHGHUL HOLLOW
by Anna Stephens

The once illustrious Gothghul family endures seasons of isolation in their castle overlooking the Hollow. But when the town is threatened by a spate of sinister manifestations, they must uncover a diabolic mystery to which they have but one clue: Mhurghast.

Unnatural Causes

Jude Reid

Martia Lyviska didn't need a diagnostor to know the man in the bed was dying.

His future was laid out before him, clear as the spread of a diviner's tarot. It was etched in the gaunt hollows of his eyes, his cracked, cyanotic lips, the rigid cords of neck muscle straining beneath his papery skin. It wouldn't be long, either. Every case of grey lung ended the same way. When the air hunger became too great for his fibrotic lungs to satisfy, desperation would turn to limb-thrashing panic, and the attending Sister Hospitaller would administer the Emperor's Mercy in the form of a large syringe of morpholox. The hospice provided care from the cradle to the grave, but they made no promises about the length of the journey.

'Martia! So sorry to keep you waiting!'

The heels of Medicae Superioris Emilja Vermannen's boots beat out a staccato rhythm on the marble as she approached, echoing around the hospice's high vaulted ceiling. In the subdued lighting, the white synthweave of her tunic glowed like the halo of an illuminated saint, the gold staff and skull of the Officio Medicae gleaming on each immaculate epaulette.

'Hello, Emilja. You're looking well.'

Fifteen years had passed since they had attended the collegio together, but Emilja's complexion was as youthful as when they first matriculated. The signs of microdosed juvenat treatment were subtle, but they were there if you knew what to look for – start early enough and you could avert the stigmata of ageing before they first began to show. Martia smoothed back the flyaway strands of her own greying hair and forced a smile onto her face.

Emilja kissed the air on either side of Martia's cheeks. 'How are you? How's Issak? Keeping well, I hope?'

'Not really.' There was nothing new about her son's condition, but that didn't make it any easier for Martia to articulate. 'I wondered – I'm sorry – I wondered if you could take another look at him. I wouldn't ask if it wasn't urgent.'

Emilja waved an expansive hand. 'I'm never too busy for Issak. Bring him in, I'd be happy to help.'

Martia glanced around the hospice. The level of bed occupancy was an accurate predictor of the current quality of the local air. 'Looks like you're full already.'

'It's never full for long. Think about it. He'd be in safe hands – you could visit every day.'

It was a tempting offer. Work would be so much easier knowing Issak was in the care of the Hospitallers, instead of her half-blind neighbour across the hall. She was on the cusp of agreeing when Emilja's meaning dawned on her.

She wasn't offering Issak admission for treatment and recovery. She was offering him a place to die.

Martia swallowed down the lump that had risen into her throat. 'No, thank you.'

'Sometimes we have to make difficult choices, that's all I'm saying.' Emilja's voice was gentle, sympathetic, knowing. 'Have you spoken to Alvar?'

'No!' The question caught Martia off balance, her reply sharper than she had intended. The thought of crawling back to Issak's father made her want to vomit. 'I can't, Em. You know that.' She glanced around the room and leaned closer, lowering her voice to a whisper. 'I wanted to ask, is there... Could you arrange another course of regeneron for him?'

'That's not easy.' Emilja shook her head ruefully.

'Please. He was so much better after last time.'

The inhaled therapy was unsanctioned, ruinously expensive and illegal without special dispensation, but Emilja's influence – and a small fortune in bribes – had been enough to secure Issak a short course. It had been worth every slate, its efficacy nothing short of miraculous. For a few months Issak had been his old self again, well enough to attend the local scholam and to celebrate his sixth birthday – but like everything else in the Thronegate, good things never lasted long. 'I'll find the slate somehow.'

Emilja's expression hovered somewhere between frustration and pity. Finally, she nodded. 'If that's what you want. But if I'm honest with you, Martia, as long as he's breathing the air in your clave, all you're doing is buying time, and not much time at that.'

The cheap chrono on Martia's wrist chimed. It was a relic of the time that Issak's daily medication had only been required at four-hourly intervals. She glanced down at it, relieved by the interruption. 'Sorry. I need to get to work.'

'I'll see what I can do. Let me know when you've got the slate together.'

'Thanks, Em. I appreciate it, really I do.'

Emilja reached out a manicured hand and touched it to the crumpled sleeve of Martia's overcoat.

'Take care of yourself.'

Martia watched her friend leave. A small, unworthy part of her wanted to shout after Emilja, to point out that the price of a single juvenat treatment would be enough to cover the cost of Issak's therapy with plenty to spare, but she bit back the words. She should be full of gratitude, not resentment. Emilja was already risking enough for their sake.

A choking sound from her left drew her attention. She turned to see that the grey-faced man was gasping, mouth gulping like a landed fish in the vain attempt to satisfy his failing lungs. At his bedside, the Sister Hospitaller's lips were moving in a silent litany, her chapped fingers drawing up a syringe of colourless liquid from a blue glass vial.

Martia made the sign of the aquila and turned to leave.

Sanguinalia was still a full month away, but already winter had settled its clammy grasp around the Thronegate. The district had been built on a spur of reclaimed land, though Alecto's south-western ocean was resolutely intent on reclaiming its stolen property. A perpetual salt wind filled the air with a pervasive damp that lingered all year round, seeping through roofs and walls, blighting everything it touched with mildew and decay. Martia pulled her cheap synthweave overcoat tighter around her shoulders and shivered.

The district's name was a reference to the void-dock in geostationary orbit above it, the long-promised gateway to the stars that would bring prosperity to the people living beneath. Within weeks of its construction, the lie had become self-evident. The only thing that Providence Station offered was back-breaking labour in hazardous conditions, its ancient Slovo IV mass-transit conveyors filling the atmosphere below full of toxic particulates as they lumbered back and forth. No one would work on Providence Station if they had a choice, just like no one would live in the Thronegate if they had anywhere else to be.

She followed the broad boulevard down to Martyr's Square, where the soot-blackened Bastion, the vladar's palace and the Officio Medicae building glared at each other across the plaza. Completing the fourth side of the square, the offices of the verispex were unobtrusive by comparison, though anywhere else in the district, the marble portico with its gilded High Gothic inscription – *Mors Mihi Lucrum* – would have shone like a one-slate piece in a midden heap.

Martia headed for the rear entrance, used by tradesmen, junior mortuarium employees and the dead. Unusually for the time of night, the perimeter gate was open, and a ground transport was sitting inside with the engine idling, its tail close to the mortuarium's roll-up steel door. She glanced up at the guard tower, the heavy gun turret barely visible in the gloom, and was dazzled a moment later by the beam of its rotating searchlight.

The groundcar had to be there on official business – there was no way the turret guard would have allowed it to enter without a permit – but something about its squat grey shape sent a prickle of unease down her spine. She took a hesitant step forward, the searchlight marking out time in indolent sweeps.

'Hello?'

She was a few yards away when the driver's door swung upwards. She stepped back, startled by the sudden movement, as a man stepped out of the vehicle, squinting as the tower's light passed over him. He was middle-aged, his city-issue coveralls straining over a once muscular physique now turning thick around the middle.

'Finally.' The man spat out the stub of a lho-stick and ground it under his boot heel. 'Thought I'd have to wait all night.'

Martia stared.

'Delivery.' He glanced down at the sheaf of papers in his hand, then offered them to Martia. 'For the personal attention of the verispex.'

'I'm not the verispex.' The thought was so ludicrous that Martia almost laughed. 'You're lucky I'm working a few extra hours tonight. We don't usually take admissions on the noctis-shift.'

She touched her seal to the control panel on the wall, and the metal door ground laboriously upward. The distinctive aroma of the mortuarium – sacred incense, preservatives and decay – drifted out into the chilly air.

'Flyer got delayed leaving Providence.' He sniffed, brushed lho-ash from the front of his shirt and opened the vehicle's rear doors. Inside the vehicle was a human corpse, sealed in an opaque plastek shroud. 'Some rogue trader shows up, jams the shipping lanes, everything grinds to a halt.'

'Give me a minute. I'll get a suspensor gurney.'

The driver shrugged. The yellow tinge to the whites of his eyes suggested his liver had seen better days. 'For his personal attention, I was told.'

'I'll make sure he gets it in the morning.'

It was unusual for the verispex to take a personal interest in an admission to the district mortuarium – in fact, it was rare for him to notice the workings of the department at all – but Martia had too much on her mind already to care about her superior's shortcomings. Once the body was transferred to the trolley and its courier had made a hasty exit, she pushed it to the elevator, closed the concertina door and pulled the lever to start the grinding descent to the dissecting chambers below.

One cadaver: male.

Circumstances of death: accident aboard void-station.

Martia flicked idly through the accompanying scrollwork as the mag-lift juddered down. The report was brief. That morning, fire had broken out in a compartment of the ship under repair – the *Caveat Emptor*, registered in the name of Lord-Captain Micah Picave – forcing an unscheduled depressurisation to prevent the blaze from spreading. This luckless individual had been the sole casualty.

Had he been dead before decompression? A glance at the shrouded body suggested otherwise. There was none of the classic posturing of immolation: back arched, arms drawn up in a pugilist's guard, muscles cooked and contracted by intense heat. He had been spared death by fire, though she wasn't sure if suffocation was much better.

The mag-lift shuddered to a halt. She pulled back the door and nudged the suspensor sled into the long tiled corridor. There were six dissecting chambers in total, all of them well insulated against heat and sound and fitted with a separate ventilation system to the rest of the building. No one wanted the grinding of bone saws or the stench of rotting tissue drifting into the lavish reception rooms upstairs. Each chamber had its own reclamation chute, through which human remains were dispatched to a sealed refrigerated container. Once the containers reached capacity, an automated transport would convey it to the city's corpse-starch factoria for final processing. In the Thronegate, only the gilded were accorded the dignity of a grave.

She selected one of the cadaver drawers at random, transferred the body from the suspensor sled to the fully extended tray and stopped. There was something strange about the way the corpse had moved, a curious, fluctuant weight that suggested liquid had leaked into the shroud around it. Curious, she ran her hand along the cadaver's flank, and fluid rippled beneath the plastek sheet. There were any number of reasons why a body might seep after death, but not usually so soon, especially not if it had been flash-frozen by exposure to the void.

Martia took a step away from the table. This was none of her business. These remains were for the verispex to deal with. No good would come of meddling in matters above her pay grade, but the temptation of the diagnostic puzzle was almost too much to resist. So much of her time at work was taken up with mindless, repetitive tasks – cleaning, filing, moving cadavers, cleaning again – but she had been a good diagnostician once, before circumstances had forced her into this dead-end job. Surely it wouldn't hurt to take a look, to see if anything of her old skills remained, to feel the satisfaction of pitting her wits against a clinical conundrum again, even if no one else would ever know? Where would be the harm?

Quickly, before she could change her mind, she slipped on a pair of skintight examination gloves and unfastened the shroud.

At a rough estimate the cadaver was less than twelve hours dead, though the cooling of the tissues made it impossible to be entirely sure. He was naked, blood and effluvium pooled on the plastek beneath him, but that wasn't what made the breath catch in her throat. He hadn't died by smoke, or flame, or decompression.

What had killed him was the neat bullet hole between his still-open eyes.

Martia's thoughts raced. A small-calibre solid projectile weapon had made the entrance wound, a ring of soot staining on the skin suggesting it had been fired at point-blank range. She slid her gloved hands behind the head, her fingertips sinking into a pulp of torn scalp, macerated cerebral tissue and shattered bone where the occiput should have been. Was this why the body had been marked for the personal attention of the verispex?

But if this was a known murder, then why the story of death by decompression, and where, for that matter, were the probators?

She studied the corpse from head to toe. It had been stripped naked, a mortuarian's Y-cut scoring the skin from clavicle to pubis, crudely sutured shut with black synthsilk. The shape of the abdomen was subtly wrong, as though more than the usual number of organs had been returned there after a hasty post-mortem examination. She worked a fingertip under the lowest loop of the suture until the loosely tied knot gave way. The stitching unravelled, and she folded back the abdominal wall like the covers of a textbook.

The corpse had been eviscerated – from the neatness of the work it had been done post-mortem. In place of the usual abdominal contents was an opaque plastek sack. Martia glanced at the door, gripped by a sudden unease. Someone had already dissected this cadaver, removed its organs and filled the space with… with what?

She opened the bag with an anatomist's care. In the harsh mortuarium light, its contents gleamed like a treasure trove: ornate brooches and necklaces, miniature replicas of exotic, off-world firearms, a curved dagger so thickly encrusted with jewels that it seemed impossible it could ever have been intended for use. She hooked a finger around a fine gold chain and pulled out a plain gold reliquary case small enough to fit in the palm of her hand, repulsed and intrigued in equal measure. Any one of these treasures had to be worth more than she would earn in a lifetime.

Acid surged into her throat. It was years since the mortuarium had made her nauseous, but the sensation was as sudden and intense as it had been on her first day at the dissecting table. She reached the metal sluice just before her stomach emptied in the first of a series of convulsive heaves. She leaned against it, doubled over and retching, until all that was left to bring up was a trickle of yellow bile. Empty and aching, she leaned her head against the cool tiled wall, shut her eyes and fought to slow her breathing, skin clammy with cold sweat.

Someone was smuggling goods through the mortuarium. The verispex was surely complicit in it, his silence bought with a healthy share of the profits. If the body had arrived on time it would already have been sent on its final journey to the corpse-starch factoria, its contents unloaded and the vessel neatly disposed of. The thought of how many times the same scene might have played out before was almost enough to make her retch again.

The golden chain was still threaded through her fingers, its fine links gleaming in the sterile lumen-light. She tipped the reliquary case's contents into her gloved palm: a signet ring embossed with a stylised corvid. The ruby set in its single eye blazed scarlet in a miniature conflagration. It was such a small thing. Valuable, certainly – not in the same league as the rest of the smuggled cargo, but enough to pay for Issak's treatment ten times over. Amongst so many other priceless treasures, it might not even be missed.

Temptation glittered in her palm. She regarded it for a moment, returned it to its case, wiped down the metal exterior and hung the chain around her neck. Carefully, she threaded a long, curved needle with a fresh length of black synthsilk and began the slow, laborious work of returning the body to the state in which she had found it, identical in every detail.

Every detail except one.

Snow was falling by the time she left the mortuarium, heavy flakes that melted into a wet grey slush as soon as they reached the ground. One landed on her lip. She licked it away by reflex, and instantly her mouth flooded with the bitterness of promethium residue. The taste was vile, but it was something to focus on, something to distract her from the suffocating anxiety constricting her chest. The guilt was an iron collar around her neck, accompanied by an awful, irrational certainty that her crime had already been discovered. The sense of unease was so strong that she could almost believe she was being watched.

She retraced her footsteps to the hospice door and found it locked. She knocked hard enough to scrape her knuckles raw, then waited so long that she started to wonder if she'd even been heard. At last there was a shuffling sound from inside, and the door swung open to reveal the young Sister Hospitaller she had noticed the evening before. Had it really only been a few hours since she had spoken with Emilja?

'Forgive me, Sister – is Medicae Superioris Vermannen still here?'

The Sister shook her head, her eyes heavy and red-rimmed. Martia felt a sudden pang of sympathy for a fellow noctis-shift worker. 'She left after her rounds.'

'Did she say where she was going? When she'd be back?'

'The evening, I think.' The Hospitaller shrugged an indifferent shoulder. She was younger than Martia, but already her face was drawn and weary, hopeless eyes deeply shadowed beneath the white wings of her headdress. Witnessing the slow death of hope every day would do that to you.

'If you see her before then, I need you to pass on a message. Ask her to go ahead and book Issak's treatment – tell her I've got the slate. Ask her to contact me as soon as she can – at home or at work. Please?'

The winged headdress nodded once. Dry-skinned hands crossed over the white-robed chest, fingers spread out like wings. 'I will. He of Terra be with you.'

'And with you, Sister,' Martia replied, though the thought of the watchful gaze of the God-Emperor served only to tighten the constricting band of guilt about her throat.

In the Thronegate, just like the rest of Varangantua, the slums were never far away. The Kuja habclave was a maze of narrow alleyways, home to hundreds of densely packed bodies. It wasn't somewhere she visited by choice, but in the last few months she had come here so often that she knew the streets by heart. Footprints suggested that she wasn't the first to visit that evening, but that was hardly a surprise. There was no shortage of desperate people in this city.

A solitary lumoglobe burned inside, illuminating a figure stooped forward over a workbench. Martia knocked once on the heavy plasteel door. It swung open without a sound, and the woman at the bench looked up with mismatched eyes – one deep-set and dark brown, the other an ornately crafted augmetic.

'Good evening, Mama.' Martia was careful to keep her voice soft, her tone deferential. The old woman might look harmless, but the mere existence of her thriving pawnshop in a clave like this attested to both her resilience and her ruthlessness.

Mama Louhi placed the delicate piece of clockwork down on her bench and turned towards the door. Her wizened face brightened in recognition. 'Back again? Slate runs through the fingers so fast, doesn't it?'

Martia plastered a smile over her desperation, knowing it wouldn't fool anyone. No one came to Mama Louhi unless they needed something badly enough to sell their pride along with whatever else they had to offer. 'I've brought something that might be of interest to you.'

'I do have many interests, that's true.'

The old woman motioned to her to sit. Martia stole a glimpse of the cabinet on the far wall, the velvet cushion inside arrayed with gaudy jewellery, pocket-sized firearms and second-hand augmetics. There was no sign of her own pawned treasures: her grandmother's betrothal ring, a necklace that Issak's father had given her when they first met, the earrings that had been a graduation present from her mother. One by one they had slipped from her hands, relics of a drowned past that could never be reclaimed.

'My son isn't well.' The smile slipped, and she didn't bother to fix it. 'Treatment is expensive.'

Martia drew the reliquary out from beneath her sodden overcoat and tipped the contents onto the table.

'May I?' Without waiting for an answer the old woman extended a gnarled hand and lifted the ring to examine it, light catching on the tiny ruby in the corvid's eye. She rose, locked the door and closed the shutters.

'Where did you get this?'

'A family heirloom.'

The pawnbroker's face quirked with amusement. 'Don't give me that groxshit.'

'If you're not interested, I'll take it somewhere else.'

'I didn't say I wasn't interested.'

Louhi lifted a bottle of expensive-looking Urgeyena slatov and poured two glasses. She knocked back the first and set the second in front of Martia in a cloud of pungent vapour. The old woman turned the ring through a full three hundred and sixty degrees, a lens telescoping outward from her augmetic eye as her attention settled on the engraved crest.

'That symbol.' She tapped the ring. 'House Picave.'

It took a moment for Martia to remember where she had read the name – the rogue trader from the incident report, the one whose ship had arrived unexpectedly at Providence Station.

'If I was the sort of person who asked questions,' Louhi said, deftly fitting an array of tinted lenses onto her augmetic, 'I'd be wondering how a rogue trader's signet found its way into your hands.' The lenses flicked up and down with dizzying speed, a tiny red diode flickering behind them. 'Luckily for you, I'm not.'

'I'm not looking for trouble.'

'No one ever is.' The machine-spirit in the augmetic eye let out a series of high-pitched chirps. Mama Louhi rotated the ring in between her fingers, the tiny corvid always facing her. The augmetic chirped again, then she put the ring down on the workbench so gently that there was no sound at all.

'Take it and get out.'

'I thought you were interested?' Martia blinked, taken aback.

Louhi shoved the ring away, and Martia scrambled to intercept it before it could hit the floor. The old woman's face had turned an ugly shade of grey. 'I've been in this game long enough to know some things are fifty times more trouble than they're worth.' She stood again, opened the door, waited expectantly for Martia to leave. 'You want my advice? Throw the Throne-damned thing in the river, try not to blow your head off doing it – and pray to the God-Emperor that no one ever finds out it passed through your hands.'

'I don't understand–'

'That's right. You don't.'

The door slammed in Martia's face. She stood stupidly on the doorstep, the ring clutched in her fist. Through the shutters she could see the silhouette of the old woman at her workbench, another shot of slatov already in her hand. Something about the ring had scared her – something more than the identity of its rightful owner.

Martia felt a tendril of that same fear caress her spine. She had been an idiot to think the ring was a simple piece of jewellery.

Louhi's reaction had said it all. There had been weapons inside the corpse – if this ring was one of them, then to be found in possession of it without a permit would be every bit as lethal as any shot it fired. She ran her thumbnail across the ring's surface, feeling for any irregularity in the metal that might indicate a firing mechanism, but found nothing.

It wasn't too late to put things right. Diurnus-shift would start in less than an hour, but she could still be back before the day's work was properly underway. She could loosen a stitch or two from the body, slip the reliquary case back inside its grisly container and reseal the body bag in seconds. No one would suspect, and she could wash her hands of the whole wretched affair.

She hurried back towards the mortuarium, resolute in her determination to see the ring gone from her hands. Though the skies were still dark, the district was coming to life around her, preparing itself for the scant few hours of thin light that were the gift of Alecto's dying sun. The snow had settled into a thick grey slush that clawed its way up her ankles as she walked. Her thoughts fell into time with the rhythm of her footsteps. *Not far to go. Not long till it's over.*

A Bulwark hurtled down the boulevard with clarions wailing, sending a spray of freezing water into the air, soaking through her overcoat and trickling into her boots. She was still standing, half frozen with cold and shock, when a pair of Rampart groundcars followed it, their white-blue lights flashing. What could have happened to draw so much attention so close to the Bastion? She picked up her pace, pulse quickening to match. The sanctioners' vehicles were heading directly for Martyr's Square, parked around the magnificent front door of the verispex's offices.

A cordon was already in place outside the building, two

sanctioners in riot armour framing the doorway. One took a step forward and raised an autogun. 'I'll have to stop you there, ma'am,' he said, his voice muffled by the visor of his helmet.

'I work here.' She fumbled the seal from her pocket. 'Adjutor Tertius Martia Lyviska. I'm... supposed to be on shift.'

'I'd thank the Emperor you were late for work, then.' The helmet tilted to one side, and the visor slid upward with a soft hydraulic hiss. The face beneath was unexpectedly young, wearing an expression composed of equal parts irritation, curiosity and contempt. His teeth were stained yellow, the unmistakable stigmata of a heavy cotin habit.

'What happened?' The fear wrapped around Martia's chest tightened its grip. She craned her neck to one side, straining to see what had happened inside the building. Blurry silhouettes moved behind the frosted armaglass door, too vague to make out any detail.

'Your guess is as good as mine, doc.' His companion shot him an irritated look, and he ignored her. 'Looks like someone showed up, ransacked the place, killed anyone who got in the way and left. Whole building's going to be cordoned off till the probators are finished. They'll probably need to send to Polaris or Bastopole for a verispex.'

'Why?' She shook her head, trying to clear her foggy thoughts.

'Well, the one in there's not going to be much use in the state he's in, is he?' The sanctioner jerked his head towards the doorway. 'Found dead in his office. Barely a mark on him, they said, but whoever did it turned the whole room upside down. Documents everywhere, cabinets broken open. Looking for something, if you ask me.'

'Lucky no one's asking you then,' his companion said, without raising her visor. Through her helmet's speakers her voice had a harsh, metallic ring. 'And you should head back to your hab, adjutor. I expect the probators will have some questions for you once they've examined the murder scene.'

Heat rushed to her face, and she shoved her shaking hands into the pockets of her overcoat, fighting to keep the fear from her voice. 'Certainly, sanctioner. Thank you.'

On the far side of the square, a dark grey Grappia Galo was drawing to a halt outside the vladar's palace. A probator's vehicle. It took all of her willpower to turn her back on the sanctioners, to walk at a leisurely pace, to ignore the voice in her head screaming at her to run. Whoever had been here had been looking for something. Something important enough to kill for.

The reliquary case burned against her skin like a convict's brand.

'Adjutor?' The helmeted sanctioner again. Should she run? There was an alley only a few yards away, but the thought of the sanctioners' autoguns was enough to stop her in her tracks. Instead, she turned, forcing a smile onto her face.

'Yes, sanctioner?'

'I'll need to take your address.'

'Suborbital clave, building one-oh-four, hab six-D.' The truth came out by reflex before it could occur to her to lie. She risked a glance at the probator's groundcar. The driver's door was open, a man in a long dark overcoat unfolding from the seat. In minutes the probator would be at the building, with questions she had no means of answering. Cold sweat trickled down her back. She swallowed. 'Will that be all, officer?'

The sanctioner nodded. 'For now, adjutor. Stay safe.'

'I will.' She forced herself to smile, every muscle locked tight as she turned to walk away. At every step she expected a hand to clamp around her shoulder and wrench her back to face justice. The mortuarium had been ransacked, the verispex murdered, and if she'd been there an hour earlier she would have shared his fate. Her chest tightened at the thought. What would have happened to Issak if she hadn't come home?

She managed to hide her panic until she had turned off Martyr's Square, then stopped and rested her back against the brick wall of the alley. *Think. Slow down and think.*

Whoever had been in the mortuarium would have had easy access to its records. If they were looking for the ring – and what else could they be searching for? – they would know who had access to the building, where they worked, their next of kin. She sped up, icy water spattering her legs, soaking through the soles of her boots. The murderer could be there in her home already, tearing apart the hab and anyone inside. She imagined her neighbour lying motionless inside a splintered door, furniture overturned, Issak's tiny body sprawled on the floor like a broken-limbed doll–

She broke into a run, heedless of the stares of the locals, and didn't stop until she was through the rust-streaked door of her hab-block. She didn't bother with the mag-lift, fear driving her up the stairs despite her burning lungs and aching legs, scanning the silent building for any trace of an intruder. The building's door had been locked, the habs she passed intact, no evidence of bullet holes or plasma discharges. Surely that had to be a good sign?

Her mind's eye was already conjuring up the splintered remains of the door as she surmounted the final flight, but the green-painted door with its rusty metal nameplate was exactly as she had left it a lifetime ago. The lock panel was glowing with its usual dull red light. She punched in her code and the door slid smoothly to one side.

'Issak?' Her voice was an unsteady whisper. 'Are you awake?'

The hab smelled the same as it always did: reheated food, disinfectant and the faint tang of sickness that pervaded every room no matter how hard and long she scrubbed. She held her breath, straining her ears to catch the soft in-and-out rattle of Issak's breathing. There was nothing but silence.

Something touched her shoulder, and she screamed and twisted away, hands flying up to shield her face.

'Martia!'

It was a voice she knew. Her neighbour from the next-door hab. Issak's babysitter.

'Martia, what's the matter?'

She fumbled along the wall until she found the lumen-switch and tapped it with a shaking hand. The hab flooded with grimy yellow light, illuminating a stooped figure, a lined face and a pair of eyes milky with cataracts.

'Rakhel – I'm sorry.' She took a deep breath, forcing down the ball of panic in her throat. 'You startled me. Is Issak with you?' It wouldn't have been the first time that Issak had decided to sleep in Aunt Rakhi's hab, the auto-nebuliser humming at his bedside.

Rakhel was shaking her head, but the expression on her weathered face was serene. 'He's gone already.'

'Gone?'

'For treatment.' The old neighbour's face creased into a gentle smile. 'I'm glad for you both.'

'When?' Martia seized her by the shoulders, panic lending force to her grip. Rakhel tried to pull back, but Martia held her tight.

'Not long – the medicae took him – I didn't think...'

'Did they say where?'

'No. I thought... I thought you knew!'

Martia shoved her neighbour away and turned to search the hab-unit. The cupboards of the refec-chamber had been emptied onto the floor. Even the door of the radiation oven was hanging open. The dorm-chamber had been subjected to the same treatment, the blankets torn from the bed, clothes strewn on the rug, and worst of all, the dreadful absence of her son, raw as an open wound.

She sat on the edge of his bed and put her head in her hands. The verispex was dead, Issak missing, and all because she had been foolish enough to steal a piece of jewellery that someone powerful and dangerous wanted back enough to kill for.

A folded piece of parchment on the bedside cabinet caught her eye, one of the cheap sheets used for notetaking in the district's hospices. She unfolded it carefully, and it released the faint smell of carbolic soap. The message inside was printed in bone-gall ink.

BRING IT TO THE MORTUARIUM. COME ALONE.

The medicae took him, Rakhel had said. She was half blind, her eyes ruined by long years of labour in the munitions manufactorum, but even she wouldn't have handed Issak over to a total stranger. Issak had gone with someone he had known, someone he trusted.

Someone whose handwriting hadn't changed since the Collegio Medicae fifteen years before.

Martyr's Square was cordoned off with heavy sanctioner's barricades when she returned, but she didn't get close enough to see how many officers were guarding the front door. Instead, she took the alleyway to the rear entrance, convinced with each step that an unseen figure would unfold from the darkness and press the muzzle of a pistol to the back of her head. The perimeter gate hung open, the tower above in darkness, though the searchlight still spun its lazy arc across the grounds. Shouldn't there be sanctioners patrolling the building so soon after a murder?

The building towered over her, the windows of the upper laboratoria empty as the eyes of a corpse. The rear door hung open, the hallway beyond in pitch darkness. She hesitated on the threshold, every muscle locked rigid, an insistent voice in her head telling her to run and not look back.

An icy line of sweat trickled down between her shoulder blades. She held the image of Issak's sleeping face in her mind as she took one halting step inside, and then another. The mortuarium mag-lift was waiting, its door drawn back, the darkness within like the throat of a monstrous beast. She stepped inside, closed the door, pulled the lever and began her juddering descent, wishing she had brought a weapon. Too late for that now.

'Hello?'

The mortuarium corridor was in darkness, the sole illumination emanating from the furthest dissecting chamber, the faint hum of a suspensor gurney niggling at the limit of her hearing.

'Issak?'

Something moved at the end of the corridor, a sharp, tapping footstep followed a moment later by Emilja's echoing voice. 'He's here, Martia. Give me the ring and you can have him back.'

'I didn't bring it. Once I know he's safe I'll tell you where it is.'

Emilja laughed. 'You're forgetting how well I know you. You always were a terrible liar. Hand it over.'

'Where's Issak?' She pressed her back to the tiled wall.

'He's with me. I wouldn't hurt him, you know that. I only want what's mine.'

'What about the verispex? Or that poor bastard you had gutted like an eel?'

She was close enough now that she could hear Emilja's sigh of frustration.

'I had nothing to do with what happened to the verispex. Someone must have found out about the cargo and decided they wanted it enough to kill him.'

'And the dock worker?'

'He'd...' Emilja paused. 'Some dispute up there got out of hand. His body ended up in the right place at the right time. He'd have been dead in a few weeks anyway. You know what life expectancy's like up there.' Her voice was gentle, authoritative, compassionate – a senior clinician delivering a difficult diagnosis. 'I'm not proud of my part in any of this, but think of everything I've done with the slate. You don't think the hospice runs on the funding it gets from the city, do you? Where's the harm in making something good out of a bad situation?'

Martia reached under her tunic for the gold chain and pulled the reliquary case over her head. 'I just want Issak back.'

'I know. Put it on the floor and slide it down the corridor.'

Martia slid the case along the floor. It skidded to a halt in the pool of light outside the furthest dissecting chamber. Emilja stepped out of the darkened room one door closer, standing between Martia and the reliquary case on the floor, a laspistol in her hand.

'Thank you,' she said, and pulled the trigger.

The corridor blazed green with las-fire. Martia hurled herself to the floor, pain searing across the right side of her neck, the air sharp with the smell of sizzling hair. Emilja's las-bolt had passed close enough for the blistering heat to cauterise a narrow second-degree burn an inch below the line of her jaw. She looked up to see Emilja raising the pistol again, the reliquary case still glittering on the ground behind her.

The empty reliquary case.

Martia uncurled her fist. The stolen signet ring lay in her palm, the corvid's one eye regarding her with a quizzical air. If she was right, it might – *might* – hold the key to getting Issak out of here alive. If she was wrong, her life expectancy would be measured in seconds. She closed her eyes, offered up a quick, wordless prayer, and pressed the jewel as hard as she could.

She felt rather than heard the tiny click of the mechanism, then a dazzlingly intense beam of blood-red light erupted from her hand. One tiled wall exploded, filling the air with dust and smoke. The ring flew from her grip to clatter across the floor. She staggered to her feet as a sickly blue-green after-image danced in front of her eyes. Somewhere in the gloom Emilja was coughing, but the smoky air hid her from sight.

The eschar covering the burn on her neck cracked as Martia groped her way into the darkened dissecting chamber, razoring a line of agony down the already throbbing wound. She aimed herself towards the hum of the suspensor unit, relief flooding through her as she heard the soft, achingly familiar sound of Issak's cough. He was there. He was alive.

She almost knocked him from the suspensor gurney as her fumbling hands found his shoulders, his face, the soft, downy curls of his hair. 'I'm here. I'm here, Issak.' He stirred as she lifted his dead weight into her arms, and she barely choked back a scream as he nestled his face into her burned neck. Emilja was moving in the corridor outside, scrabbling through the rubble, no doubt searching for the ring. Martia only hoped she had dropped the laspistol as well.

The mag-lift was only a few yards away. If she was quick, if the God-Emperor was willing, she and Issak could be inside before the air cleared, before Emilja could aim and shoot again. Martia readied herself to run – and then froze as a muffled impact struck the cage of the elevator. Something – or someone – had landed on top of it.

The scrabbling from outside the room stopped.

'What in the warp? I told you to come alone, Martia. Did you... Did you tell the sanctioners?'

Martia held her breath. The sound of shearing metal echoed down the corridor, devastatingly loud in the silence. Whoever had arrived was ripping through the roof of the mag-lift, someone who had been waiting in the shadows outside the building. Someone who had taken care of the sanctioners patrolling outside.

'I suppose you think you're clever,' Emilja said. Was that an edge of fear creeping into her voice? 'But you're not. You're a fool, Martia. You always have been.'

The metal gave way with a final shriek, and someone dropped to the ground. Martia bit her lip hard enough that she tasted blood. There was nowhere to run. She kissed the top of Issak's head, opened the nearest cadaver drawer – empty, thank the Throne, it was empty – placed him lovingly inside and slid it shut.

Martia pressed her back against the wall, wrapped her arms around her chest and waited.

One soft footstep, then another. Emilja discharged her las-pistol again, the dust particles diffusing the light into a vivid green cloud.

Another shot. Another footstep. 'Wait – you can have it! Here!' Emilja's voice was full of panic now. The footsteps stopped. 'Here. Here it is. Take it.'

There was a soft hiss, followed a split second later by an impact so quiet Martia almost missed it, an exhalation of breath, long and slow, then the thud of something heavy hitting the ground.

A vox-unit crackled.

'I have it, lord-captain.' The voice was distorted and mechanical, the Low Gothic spoken with a heavy off-world accent. 'Discharged, as detected, but otherwise undamaged. Threat neutralised.' A short, derisive sniff. 'Such as it was.'

Through the open doorway, she caught sight of a lithe figure in a close-fitting black bodyglove, the helmeted head a featureless mask. In one hand it held a needle pistol, the ornate grip shaped like the head of a ruby-eyed corvid.

Martia closed her eyes.

'No, lord-captain.' The intruder almost sounded disappointed. 'No one left worth bothering with.'

Time stretched into a single endless moment.

When at last she opened her eyes, the mortuarium was empty.

Unsteadily, she pulled herself to her feet, lifted Issak from his hiding place and lowered him clumsily to the ground. His eyes had opened, but his gaze was fixed on a distant point that only he could see. He coughed, drew a deep, wheezing breath, then coughed again, his fragile body racked with the effort.

Martia's relief was short-lived, eroded almost immediately by a creeping tide of despair. The ring was lost. Emilja was dead, all chance of affording Issak's treatment gone. A new verispex would be appointed, ready to assume their predecessor's role in the smuggling enterprise. Emilja would be replaced in the Officio Medicae – just another corpse chewed up in the city's insatiable jaws. And worst of all, in a month or two Issak would be dead, his irreplaceable mortal remains rendered down for nutrients, and only his mother would notice or care.

Everything was hopeless.

She tilted her head back, staring past the rows of dissecting tables at the sterile tiled wall and the hatch of the reclamation chute.

The idea, when it came, was enough to bring bile into the back of her throat. The deed would be appalling, unthinkable, but what did she have left to lose? Didn't she owe it to her son to risk everything on one final roll of the dice, a last chance at a future for them both?

'You have a sleep, Issi.' She bundled up her coat and tucked it around him, the same way she had swaddled him as a tiny baby. 'We'll go home soon.'

A tiny pinprick on Emilja's cheek was the only trace of the weapon that had killed her. Her face was frozen in a rictus of agony as Martia lifted her onto the dissecting table, but her skin was as soft and smooth as a newborn's. The juvenat treatment had fulfilled its promise. Emilja had gone to her death unblemished and beautiful.

Carefully, so as not to disturb her sleeping son, Martia laid out the tools of her trade, tested each in turn until she was ready to put scalpel to skin.

She had a message to send down the reclamation chute, and her old friend would deliver it for her.

Emilja owed her that much at least.

It was amazing what the application of enough slate could do, Martia thought, as she entered the offices of the verispex by the front door. The air inside smelled fresh and clean, the recent repairs complete and the freshly gilded inscription on the keystone possessed of a new and personal significance.

Mors Mihi Lucrum. Death enriches me.

She didn't plan to stay long at work today. Issak was expected home later, and she wanted to be there to show him their new hab with its view of the sea, far from the mass-transit conveyors and their toxic exhaust fumes.

Her personal secretary nodded a polite good morning as she passed. 'There's someone waiting for you at the rear door, ma'am. Says he's here to see you personally.'

She quickened her step, the old unease tightening in the pit of her stomach. The man was standing outside the door. His back was to her, but there was something familiar about the slope of the shoulders, the sagging midriff and the crumpled Thronegate-issue coveralls. Two corpses in the back of the vehicle this time, stiff in their white plastek shrouds.

'Delivery for your personal attention,' he said, and offered her a data-slate. The jaundice had spread from his eyes to tint the skin of his face a bilious yellow, and there was a fresh scribble of thread veins across his nose and cheeks. In a few months he'd be back at the mortuarium door, but not as a delivery driver.

'Is everything in order, verispex?'

She looked from the driver to the corpses then back again. She forced herself not to think about what was inside. Her new life – Issak's life – had come at a price, and there was no place in that life for regrets.

Martia Lyviska, newly appointed verispex of the Thronegate, took the offered data-slate and nodded.

'Thank you. Everything's in order.'

YOUR NEXT READ

BLOODLINES
by Chris Wraight

An investigation into a missing member of a wealthy family leads Probator Agusto Zidarov into a web of lies and danger amidst the criminal cartels of Varangantua. As the net closes in, Zidarov falls further into darkness from which he may never return…

For these stories and more, go to **blacklibrary.com**, **games-workshop.com**, Games Workshop and Warhammer stores, all good book stores or visit one of the thousands of independent retailers worldwide, which can be found at **games-workshop.com/storefinder**

ABOUT THE AUTHORS

Justin D Hill is the author of the Warhammer 40,000 novels *Cadia Stands, Cadian Honour* and *Traitor Rock*. He has also written the Necromunda novel *Terminal Overkill*, the Space Marine Battles novel *Storm of Damocles*, as well as the short stories 'Last Step Backwards', 'Lost Hope', 'The Battle of Tyrok Fields' and many more. His novels have won a number of prizes, as well as being *Washington Post* and *Sunday Times* Books of the Year. He lives ten miles uphill from York, where he is indoctrinating his four children in the 40K lore.

Noah Van Nguyen is a freelance writer who lives in the U.S. with his wife. His tales set in the Mortal Realms include the short story 'Monsters', and the novella *Nadir* from the Warhammer Underworlds anthology *Harrowdeep*. He has also written several stories set in the grim darkness of the 41st millennium, including 'No Third Chance', which featured in the Warhammer Crime anthology *Broken City*, and 'The Last Crucible'. When he's not writing, Noah enjoys studying foreign languages and exploring far-off lands with his wife.

Michael F Haspil is the author of the award-winning novel *Graveyard Shift* and numerous short stories. He is an avid tabletop gamer and podcaster. He was born in the 1900s and lives in beautiful Colorado with his wife and two pit bulls.

David Annandale is the author of the Warhammer Horror novels *The House of Night and Chain* and *The Deacon of Wounds,* as well as the novella *The Faith and the Flesh,* which features in the portmanteau *The Wicked and the Damned.* His work for the Horus Heresy series includes the novels *Ruinstorm* and *The Damnation of Pythos,* and the Primarchs novels *Roboute Guilliman: Lord of Ultramar* and *Vulkan: Lord of Drakes.* For Warhammer 40,000 he has written *Ephrael Stern: The Heretic Saint, Warlord: Fury of the God-Machine,* the Yarrick series, and several stories involving the Grey Knights, as well as titles for The Beast Arises and the Space Marine Battles series. For Warhammer Age of Sigmar he has written *A Dynasty of Monsters* and the Neferata titles *Mortarch of Blood* and *The Dominion of Bones.* David lectures at a Canadian university, on subjects ranging from English literature to horror films and video games.

Jude Reid lives in Glasgow with her husband and two daughters, and writes in the narrow gaps between full-time work as a surgeon, wrangling her kids and failing to tire out a border collie. In what little free time she has, she enjoys tabletop roleplaying, ITF Tae Kwon Do and inadvisably climbing big hills.

An extract from
Avenging Son
by Guy Haley

'I was there at the Siege of Terra,' Vitrian Messinius would say in his later years.

'I was there...' he would add to himself, his words never meant for ears but his own. 'I was there the day the Imperium died.'

But that was yet to come.

'To the walls! To the walls! The enemy is coming!' Captain Messinius, as he was then, led his Space Marines across the Penitent's Square high up on the Lion's Gate. 'Another attack! Repel them! Send them back to the warp!'

Thousands of red-skinned monsters born of fear and sin scaled the outer ramparts, fury and murder incarnate. The mortals they faced quailed. It took the heart of a Space Marine to stand against them without fear, and the Angels of Death were in short supply.

'Another attack, move, move! To the walls!'

They came in the days after the Avenging Son returned, emerging from nothing, eight legions strong, bringing the bulk of their numbers to bear against the chief entrance to the Imperial Palace. A decapitation strike like no other, and it came perilously close to success.

Messinius' Space Marines ran to the parapet edging the Penitent's Square. On many worlds, the square would have been a plaza fit to adorn the centre of any great city. Not on Terra. On the immensity of the Lion's Gate, it was nothing, one of hundreds of similarly huge spaces. The word 'gate' did not suit the scale of the cityscape. The Lion's Gate's bulk marched up into the sky, step by titanic step, until it rose far higher than the mountains it had supplanted. The gate had been built by the Emperor Himself, they said. Myths detailed the improbable supernatural feats required to raise it. They were lies, all of them, and belittled the true effort needed to build such an edifice. Though the Lion's Gate was made to His design and by His command, the soaring monument had been constructed by mortals, with mortal hands and mortal tools. Messinius wished that had been remembered. For men to build this was far more impressive than any godly act of creation. If men could remember that, he believed, then perhaps they would remember their own strength.

The uncanny may not have built the gate, but it threatened to bring it down. Messinius looked over the rampart lip, down to the lower levels thousands of feet below and the spread of the Anterior Barbican.

Upon the stepped fortifications of the Lion's Gate was armour of every colour and the blood of every loyal primarch. Dozens of regiments stood alongside them. Aircraft filled the sky. Guns boomed from every quarter. In the churning redness on the great roads, processional ways so huge they were akin to prairies cast in rockcrete, were flashes of gold where the Emperor's Custodian Guard battled. The might of the Imperium was gathered there, in the palace where He dwelt.

There seemed moments on that day when it might not be enough.

The outer ramparts were carpeted in red bodies that writhed and heaved, obscuring the great statues adorning the defences and covering over the guns, an invasive cancer consuming reality. The enemy were legion. There were too many foes to defeat by plan and ruse. Only guns, and will, would see the day won, but the defenders were so pitifully few.

Messinius called a wordless halt, clenched fist raised, seeking the best place to deploy his mixed company, veterans all of the Terran Crusade. Gunships and fighters sped overhead, unleashing deadly light and streams of bombs into the packed daemonic masses. There were innumerable cannons crammed onto the gate, and they all fired, rippling the structure with false earthquakes. Soon the many ships and orbital defences of Terra would add their guns, targeting the very world they were meant to guard, but the attack had come so suddenly; as yet they had had no time to react.

The noise was horrendous. Messinius' audio dampers were at maximum and still the roar of ordnance stung his ears. Those humans that survived today would be rendered deaf. But he would have welcomed more guns, and louder still, for all the defensive fury of the assailed palace could not drown out the hideous noise of the daemons – their sighing hisses, a billion serpents strong, and chittering, screaming wails. It was not only heard but sensed within the soul, the realms of spirit and of matter were so intertwined. Messinius' being would be forever stained by it.

Tactical information scrolled down his helmplate, near environs only. He had little strategic overview of the situation. The vox-channels were choked with a hellish screaming that made communication impossible. The noosphere was disrupted by etheric backwash spilling from the immaterial rifts the daemons poured through. Messinius was used to operating on his own.

Small-scale, surgical actions were the way of the Adeptus Astartes, but in a battle of this scale, a lack of central coordination would lead inevitably to defeat. This was not like the first Siege, where his kind had fought in Legions.

He called up a company-wide vox-cast and spoke to his warriors. They were not his Chapter-kin, but they would listen. The primarch himself had commanded that they do so.

'Reinforce the mortals,' he said. 'Their morale is wavering. Position yourselves every fifty yards. Cover the whole of the south-facing front. Let them see you.' He directed his warriors by chopping at the air with his left hand. His right, bearing an inactive power fist, hung heavily at his side. 'Assault Squad Antiocles, back forty yards, single firing line. Prepare to engage enemy breakthroughs only on my mark. Devastators, split to demi-squads and take up high ground, sergeant and sub-squad prime's discretion as to positioning and target. Remember our objective, heavy infliction of casualties. We kill as many as we can, we retreat, then hold at the Penitent's Arch until further notice. Command squad, with me.'

Command squad was too grand a title for the mismatched crew Messinius had gathered around himself. His own officers were light years away, if they still lived.

'Doveskamor, Tidominus,' he said to the two Aurora Marines with him. 'Take the left.'

'Yes, captain,' they voxed, and jogged away, their green armour glinting orange in the hell-light of the invasion.

The rest of his scratch squad was comprised of a communications specialist from the Death Spectres, an Omega Marine with a penchant for plasma weaponry, and a Raptor holding an ancient standard he'd taken from a dusty display.

'Why did you take that, Brother Kryvesh?' Messinius asked, as they moved forward.

'The palace is full of such relics,' said the Raptor. 'It seems only right to put them to use. No one else wanted it.'

Messinius stared at him.

'What? If the gate falls, we'll have more to worry about than my minor indiscretion. It'll be good for morale.'

The squads were splitting to join the standard humans. Such was the noise many of the men on the wall had not noticed their arrival, and a ripple of surprise went along the line as they appeared at their sides. Messinius was glad to see they seemed more firm when they turned their eyes back outwards.

'Anzigus,' he said to the Death Spectre. 'Hold back, facilitate communication within the company. Maximum signal gain. This interference will only get worse. See if you can get us patched in to wider theatre command. I'll take a hardline if you can find one.'

'Yes, captain,' said Anzigus. He bowed a helm that was bulbous with additional equipment. He already had the access flap of the bulky vox-unit on his arm open. He withdrew, the aerials on his power plant extending. He headed towards a systems nexus on the far wall of the plaza, where soaring buttresses pushed back against the immense weight bearing down upon them.

Messinius watched him go. He knew next to nothing about Anzigus. He spoke little, and when he did, his voice was funereal. His Chapter was mysterious, but the same lack of familiarity held true for many of these warriors, thrown together by miraculous events. Over their years lost wandering in the warp, Messinius had come to see some as friends as well as comrades, others he hardly knew, and none he knew so well as his own Chapter brothers. But they would stand together. They were Space Marines. They had fought by the returned primarch's side, and in that they shared a bond. They would not stint in their duty now.

Messinius chose a spot on the wall, directing his other veterans to left and right. Kryvesh he sent to the mortal officer's side. He looked down again, out past the enemy and over the outer palace. Spires stretched away in every direction. Smoke rose from all over the landscape. Some of it was new, the work of the daemon horde, but Terra had been burning for weeks. The Astronomican had failed. The galaxy was split in two. Behind them in the sky turned the great palace gyre, its deep eye marking out the throne room of the Emperor Himself.

'Sir!' A member of the Palatine Guard shouted over the din. He pointed downwards, to the left. Messinius followed his wavering finger. Three hundred feet below, daemons were climbing. They came upwards in a triangle tipped by a brute with a double rack of horns. It clambered hand over hand, far faster than should be possible, flying upwards, as if it touched the side of the towering gate only as a concession to reality. A Space Marine with claw locks could not have climbed that fast.

'Soldiers of the Imperium! The enemy is upon us!'

He looked to the mortals. Their faces were blanched with fear. Their weapons shook. Their bravery was commendable nonetheless. Not one of them attempted to run, though a wave of terror preceded the unnatural things clambering up towards them.

'We shall not turn away from our duty, no matter how fearful the foe, or how dire our fates may be,' he said. 'Behind us is the Sanctum of the Emperor Himself. As He has watched over you, now it is your turn to stand in guardianship over Him.'

The creatures were drawing closer. Through a sliding, magnified window on his display, Messinius looked into the yellow and cunning eyes of their leader. A long tongue lolled permanently from the thing's mouth, licking at the wall, tasting the terror of the beings it protected.

Boltgun actions clicked. His men leaned over the parapet,

towering over the mortals as the Lion's Gate towered over the Ultimate Wall. A wealth of targeting data was exchanged, warrior to warrior, as each chose a unique mark. No bolt would be wasted in the opening fusillade. They could hear the creatures' individual shrieks and growls, all wordless, but their meaning was clear: blood, blood, blood. Blood and skulls.

Messinius sneered at them. He ignited his power fist with a swift jerk. He always preferred the visceral thrill of manual activation. Motors came to full life. Lightning crackled around it. He aimed downwards with his bolt pistol. A reticule danced over diabolical faces, each a copy of all the others. These things were not real. They were not alive. They were projections of a false god. The Librarian Atramo had named them maladies. A spiritual sickness wearing ersatz flesh.

He reminded himself to be wary. Contempt was as thick as any armour, but these things were deadly, for all their unreality.

He knew. He had fought the Neverborn many times before.

'While He lives,' Messinius shouted, boosting his voxmitter gain to maximal, 'we stand!'

'For He of Terra!' the humans shouted, their battle cry loud enough to be heard over the booming of guns.

'For He of Terra,' said Messinius. 'Fire!' he shouted.

The Space Marines fired first. Boltguns spoke, spitting spikes of rocket flare into the foe. Bolts slammed into daemon bodies, bursting them apart. Black viscera exploded away. Black ichor showered those coming after. The daemons' false souls screamed back whence they came, though their bones and offal tumbled down like those of any truly living foe.

Las-beams speared next, and the space between the wall top and the scaling party filled with violence. The daemons were unnaturally resilient, protected from death by the energies of the warp, and though many were felled, others weathered the fire, and clambered up still, unharmed and uncaring of their dead. Messinius no longer needed his helm's magnification to see into the daemon champion's eyes. It stared at him, its smile a promise of death. The terror that preceded them was replaced by the urge to violence, and that gripped them all, foe and friend. The baseline humans began to lose their discipline. A man turned and shot his comrade, and was shot down in turn. Kryvesh banged the foot of his borrowed banner and called them back into line. Elsewhere, his warriors sang; not their Chapter warsongs, but battle hymns known to all. Wavering human voices joined them. The feelings of violence abated, just enough.

Then the things were over the parapet and on them. Messinius saw Tidominus carried down by a group of daemons, his unit signum replaced by a mortis rune in his helm. The enemy champion was racing at him. Messinius emptied his bolt pistol into its face, blowing half of it away into a fine mist of daemonic ichor. Still it leapt, hurling itself twenty feet over the parapet. Messinius fell back, keeping the creature in sight, targeting skating over his helmplate as the machine-spirit tried to maintain a target lock. Threat indicators trilled, shifting up their priority spectrum.

The daemon held up its enormous gnarled hands. Smoke whirled in the space between, coalescing into a two-handed sword almost as tall as Messinius. By the time its hoofed feet cracked the paving slabs of the square, the creature's weapon was solid. Vapour streaming from its ruined face, it pointed the broadsword at Messinius and hissed a wordless challenge.

'Accepted,' said Messinius, and moved in to attack.